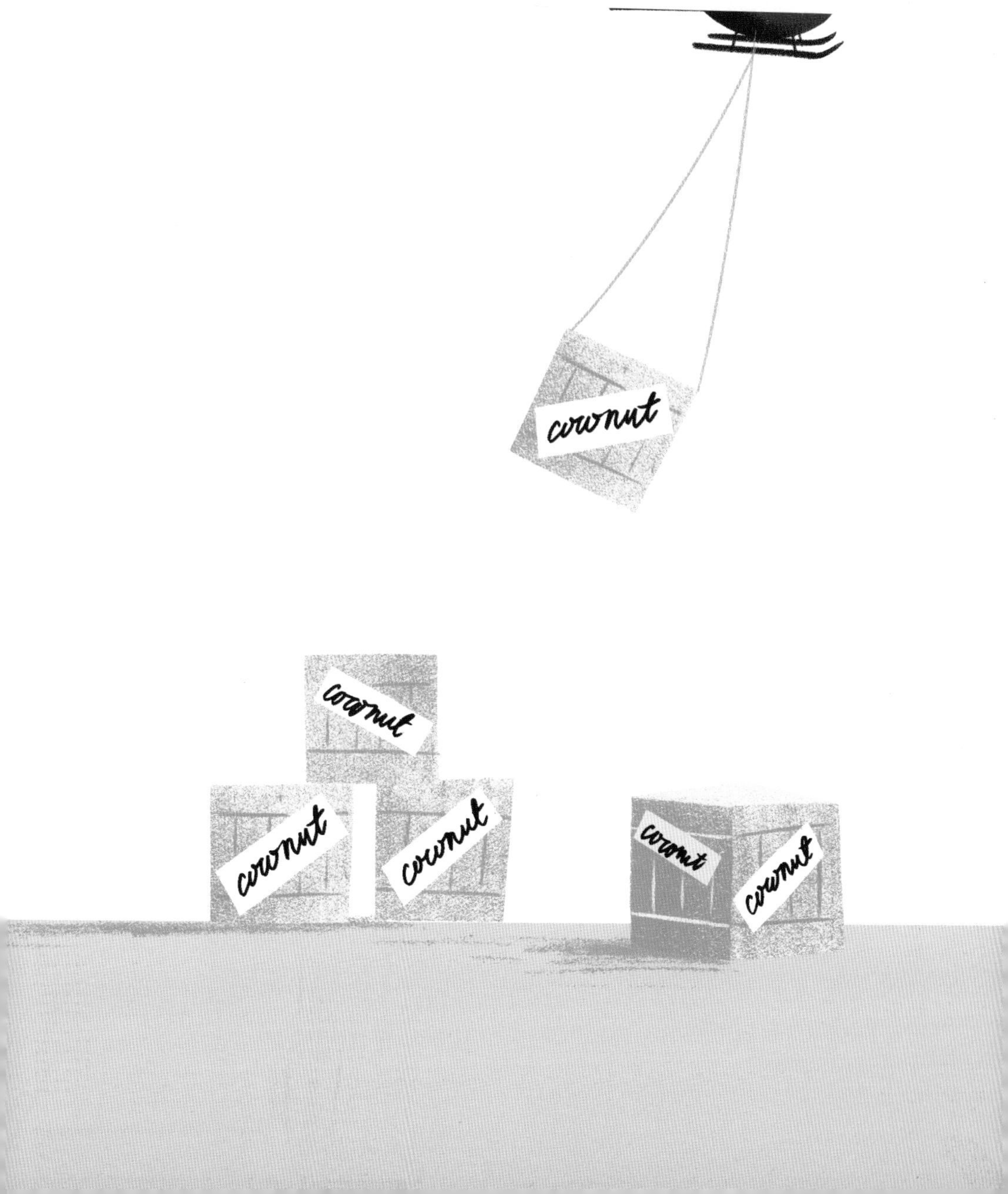
coconut
coconut
coconut
coconut
coconut
coconut

Also look for:

BOBO AND PUP-PUP: WE LOVE BUBBLES!

BOBO AND PUP-PUP: LET'S MAKE CAKE!

BOBO AND PUP-PUP: THE FUNNY BOOK

BOBO and PUP-PUP

HATCH AN EGG

by Vikram Madan
illustrated by Nicola Slater

A STEPPING STONE BOOK™

Random House 🏠 New York

For Rohit
—V.M.

To Leo and Finn
—N.S.

Text copyright © 2023 by Vikram Madan
Cover art and interior illustrations copyright © 2023 by Nicola Slater

All rights reserved. Published in the United States by Random House Children's Books,
a division of Penguin Random House LLC, New York.

Random House and the colophon are registered trademarks and A Stepping Stone Book
and the colophon are trademarks of Penguin Random House LLC.
RH Graphic with the book design is a trademark of Penguin Random House LLC.

Visit us on the Web!
rhcbooks.com

Educators and librarians, for a variety of teaching tools, visit us at RHTeachersLibrarians.com

Library of Congress Cataloging-in-Publication Data is available upon request.
ISBN 978-0-593-56284-0 (trade) | ISBN 978-0-593-56285-7 (library binding) |
ISBN 978-0-593-56286-4 (ebook)

MANUFACTURED IN CHINA
10 9 8 7 6 5 4 3 2 1
First Edition

Contents

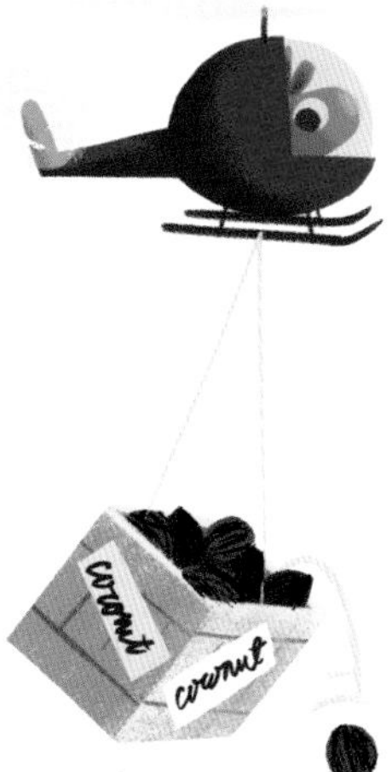

coconut
coconut

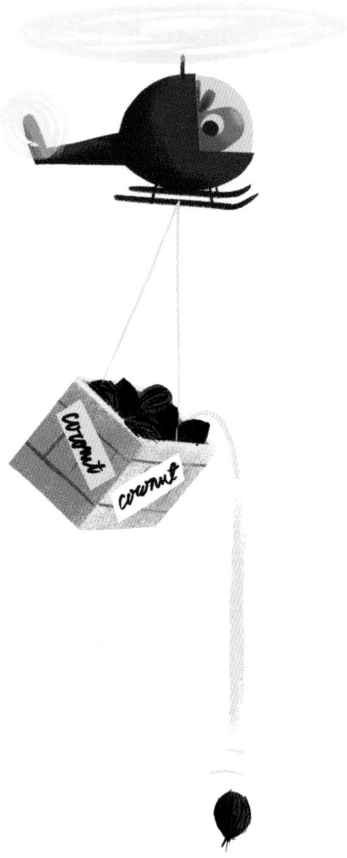
coconut
coconut

Chapter 1
The Egg

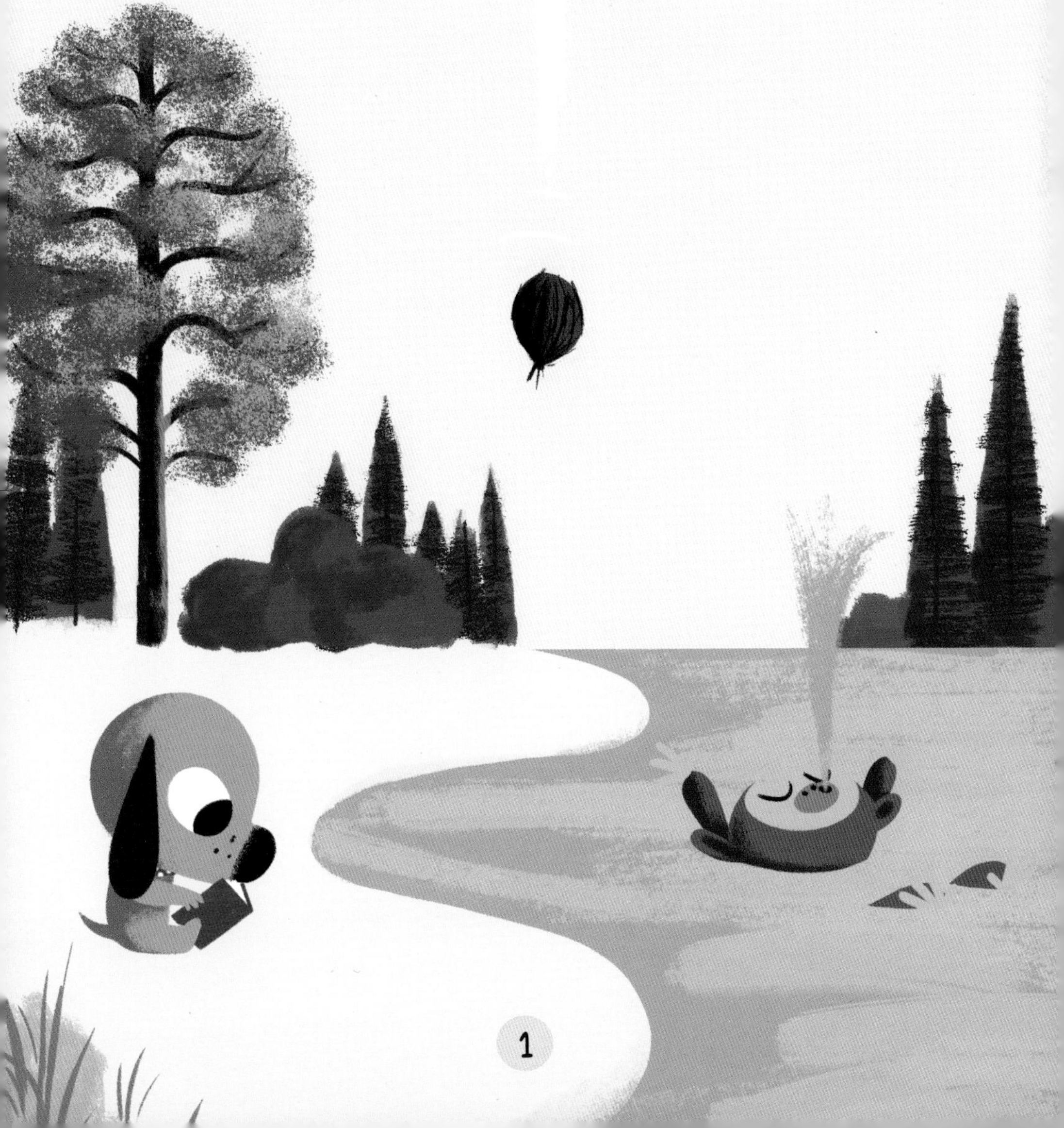

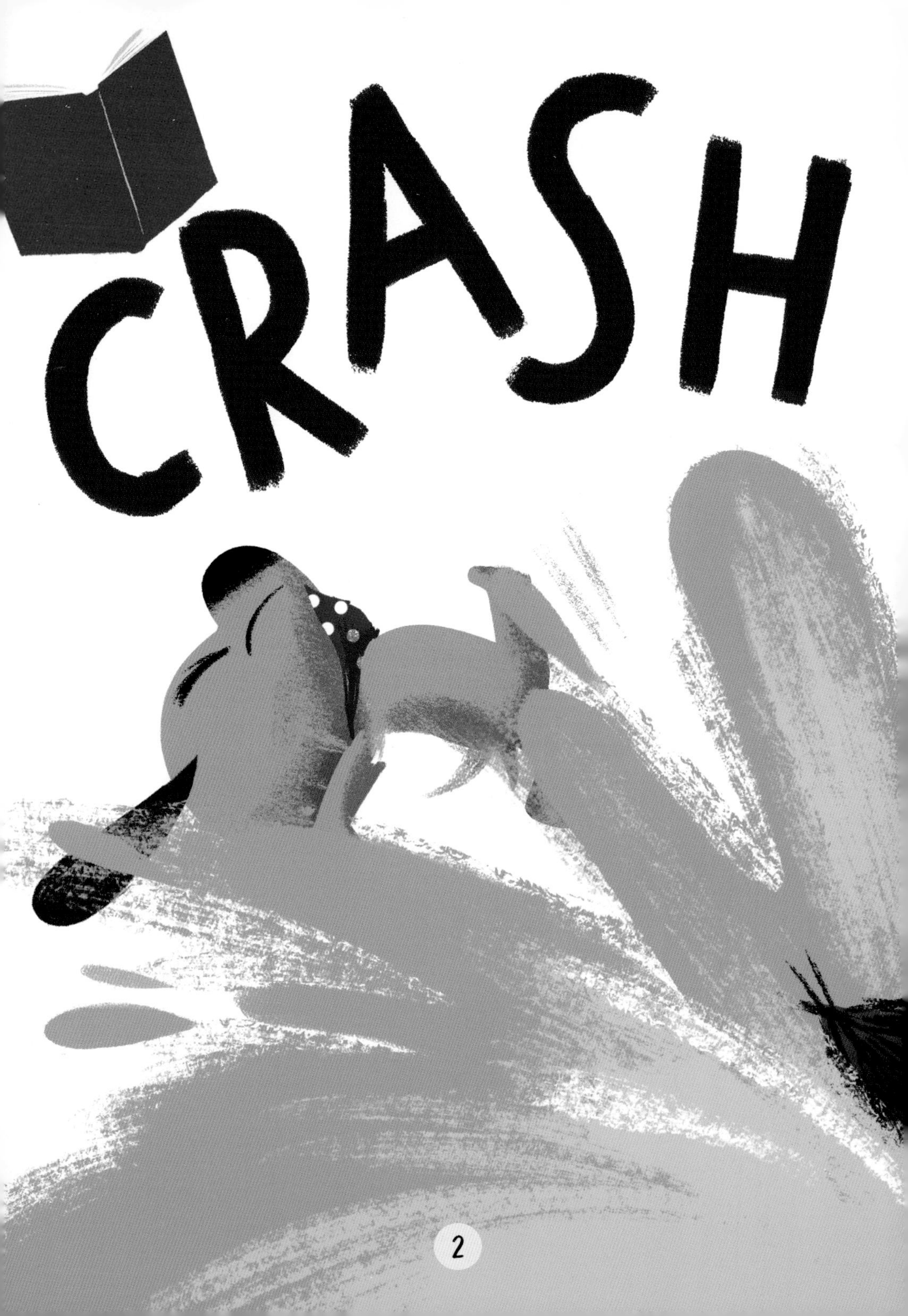
CRASH

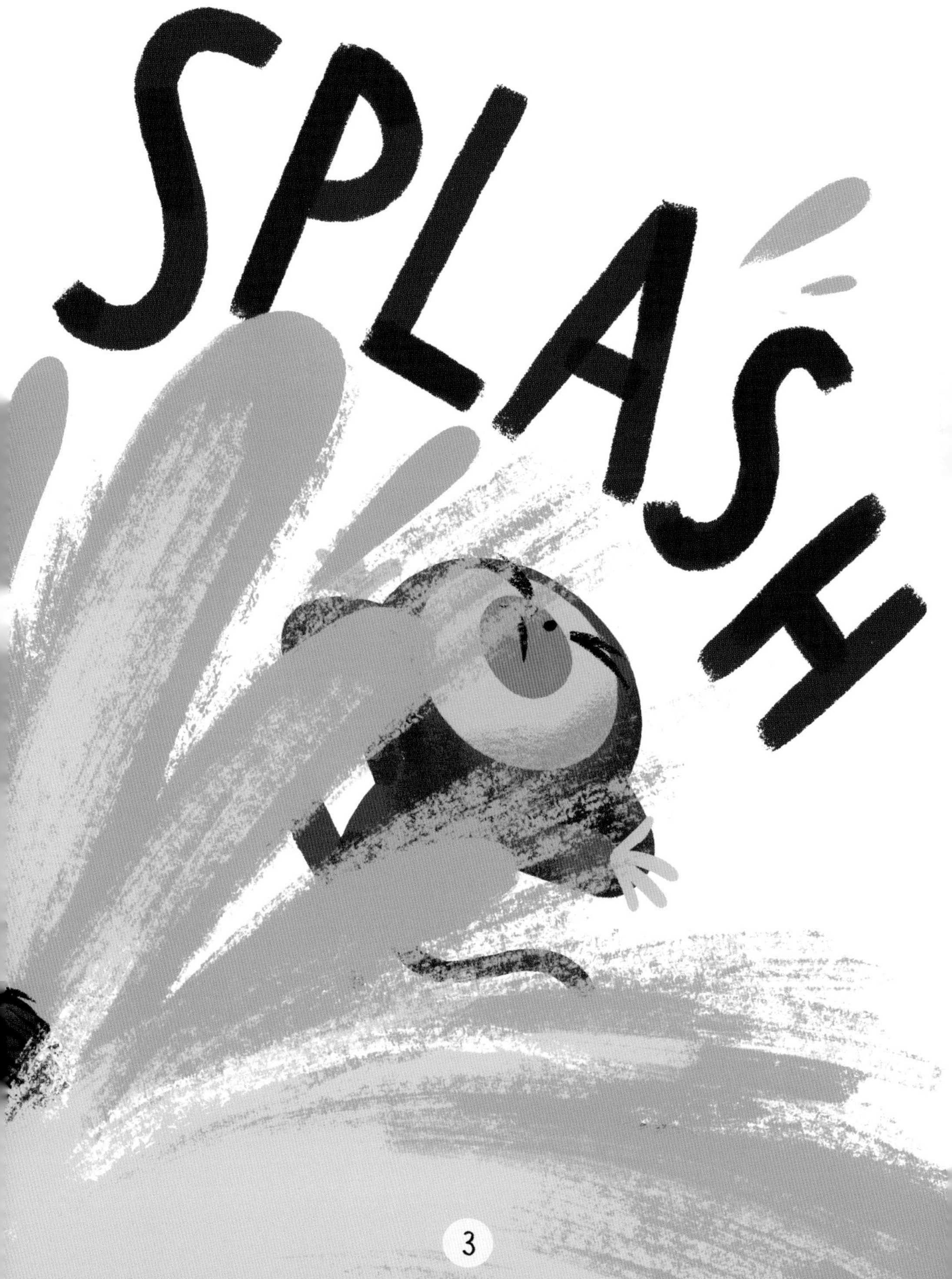
SPLASH

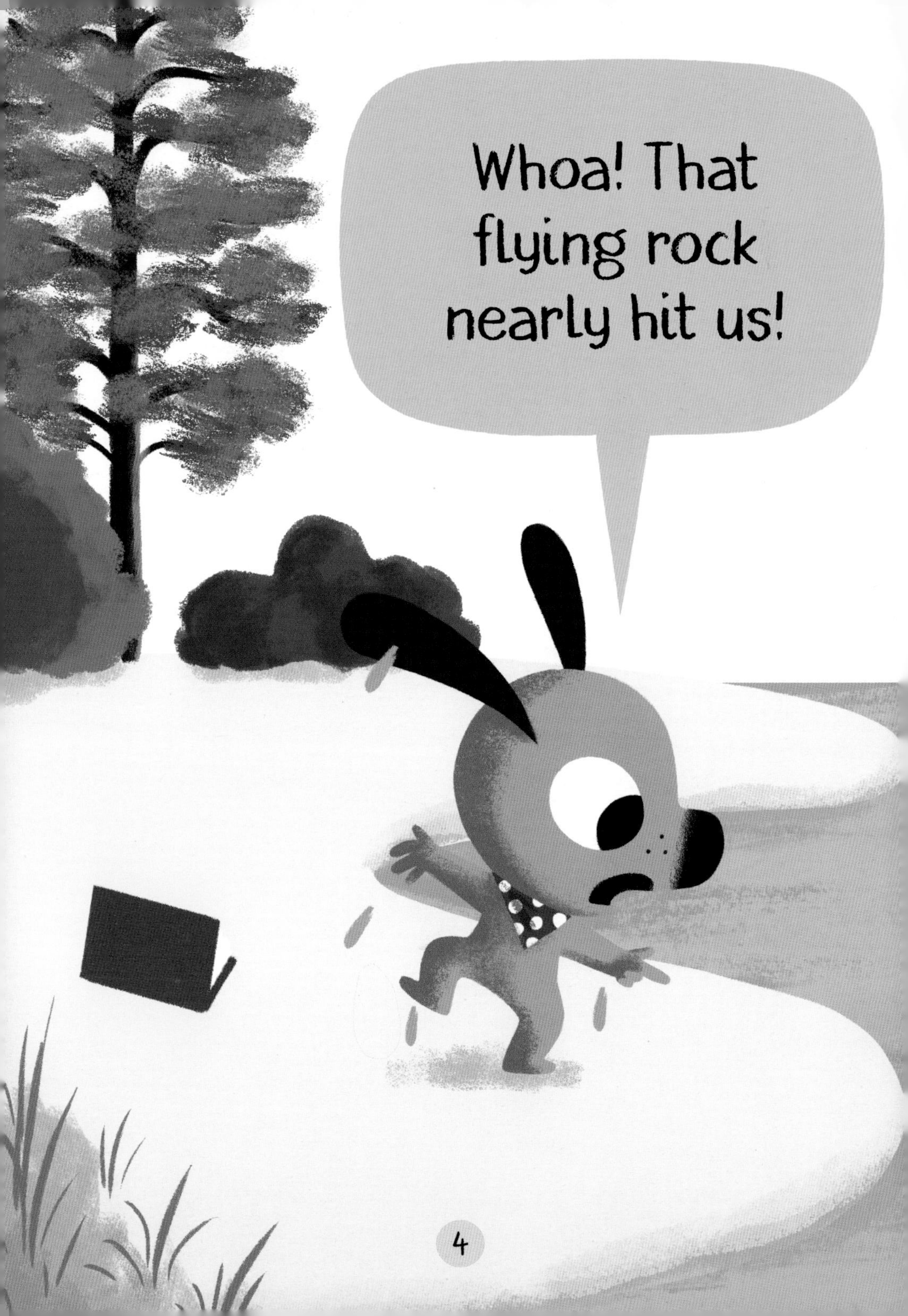
Whoa! That flying rock nearly hit us!

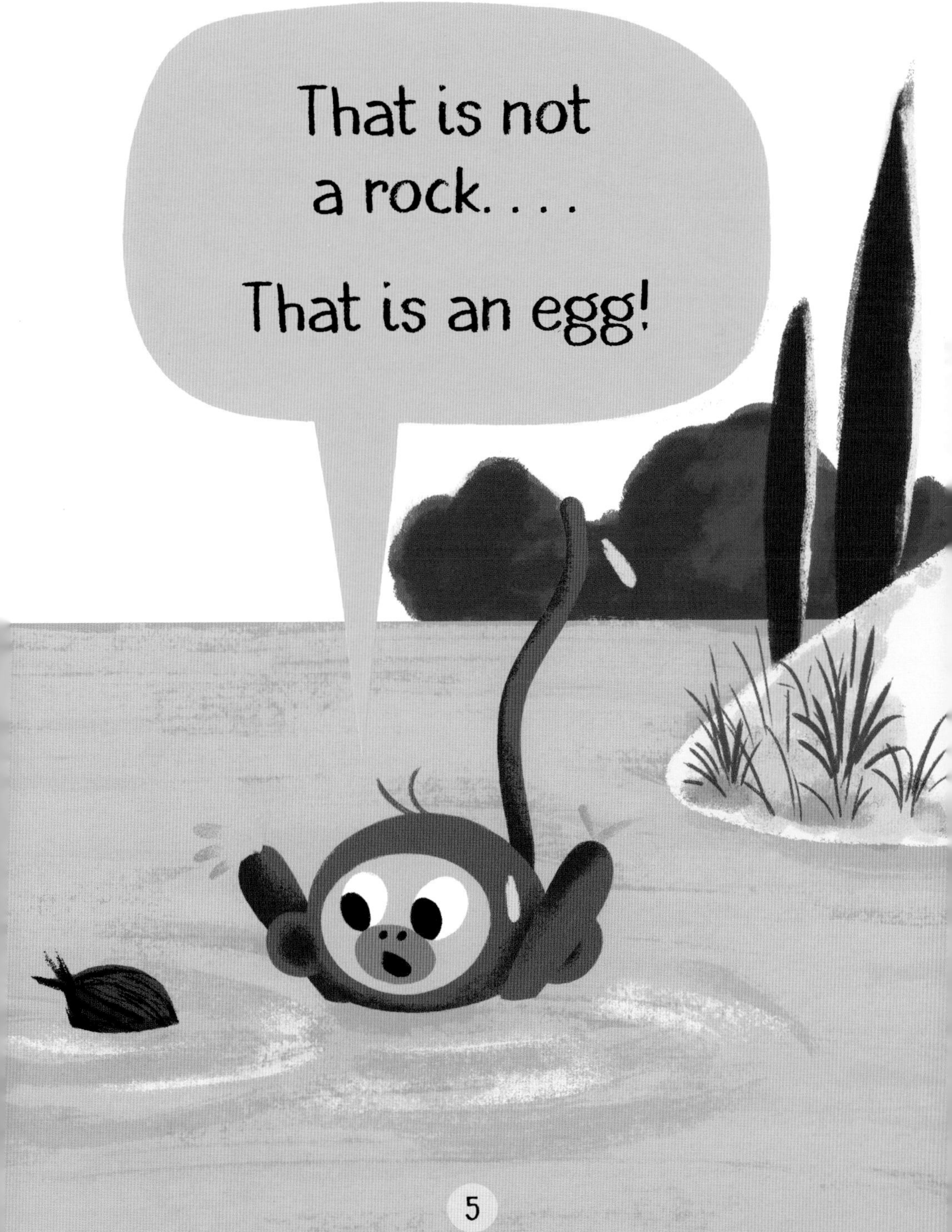
That is not
a rock. . . .
That is an egg!

Egg?!? What kind of egg is brown and fuzzy?

Easy!
A BEAR egg!

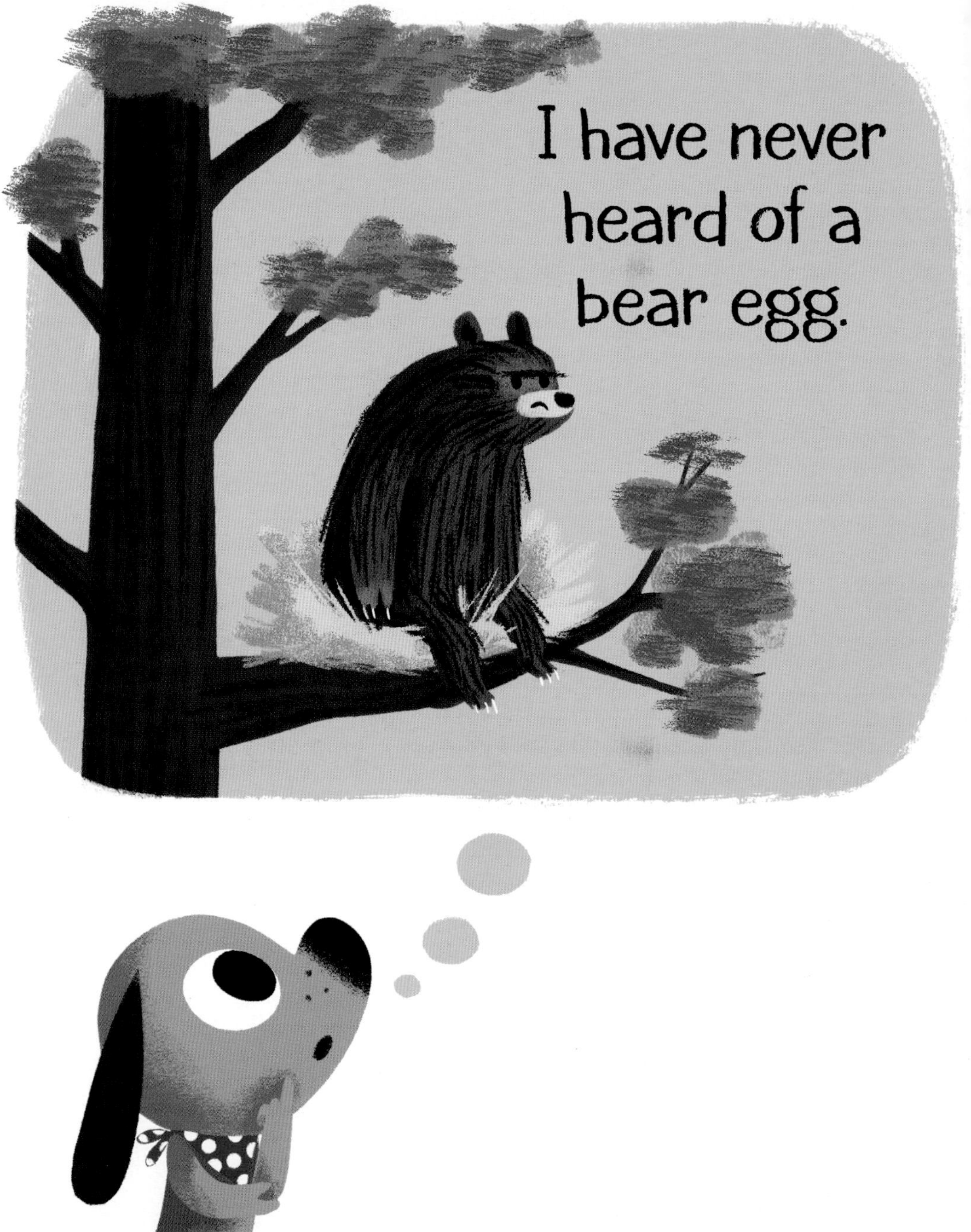
I have never heard of a bear egg.

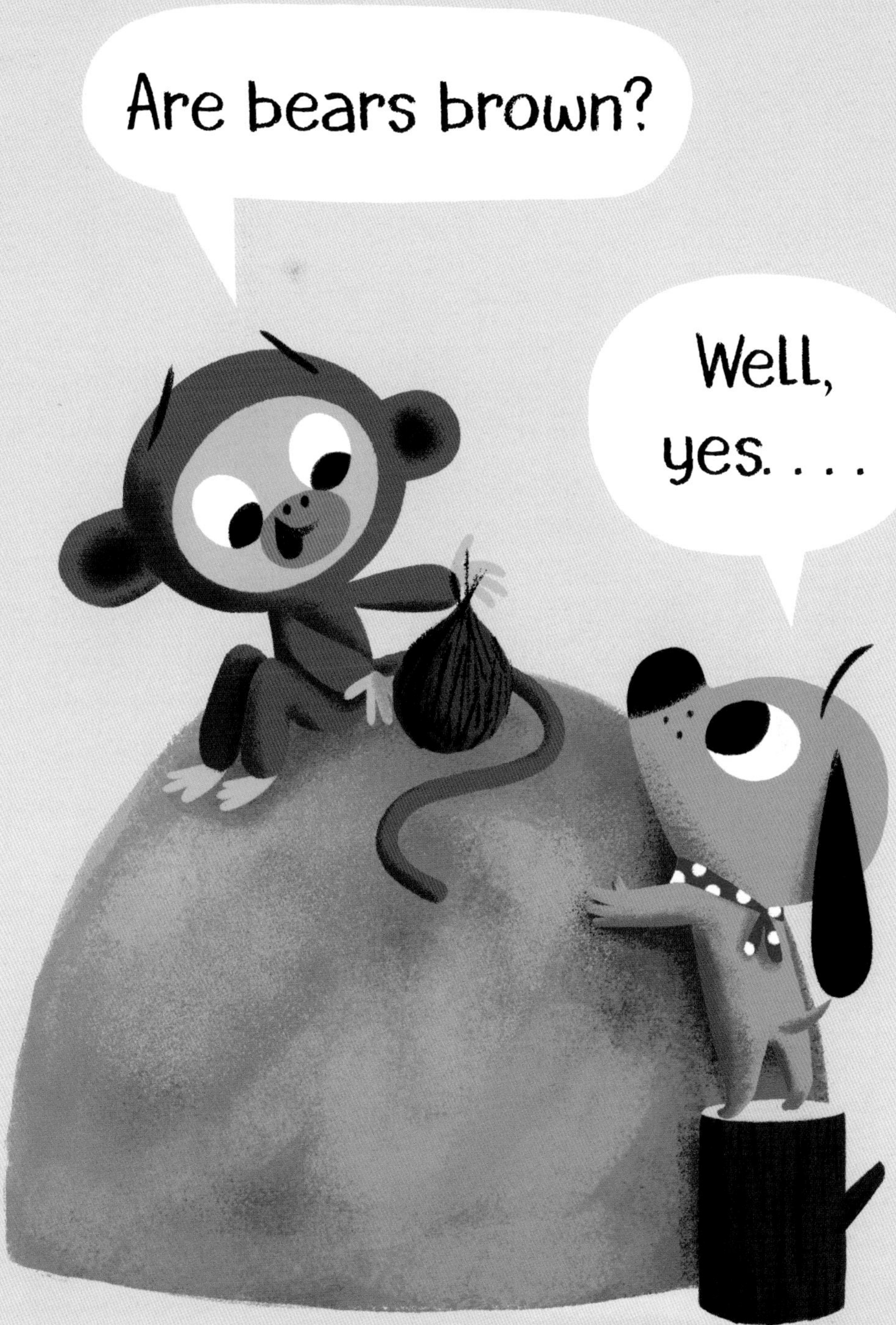
Are bears brown?
Well, yes. . . .

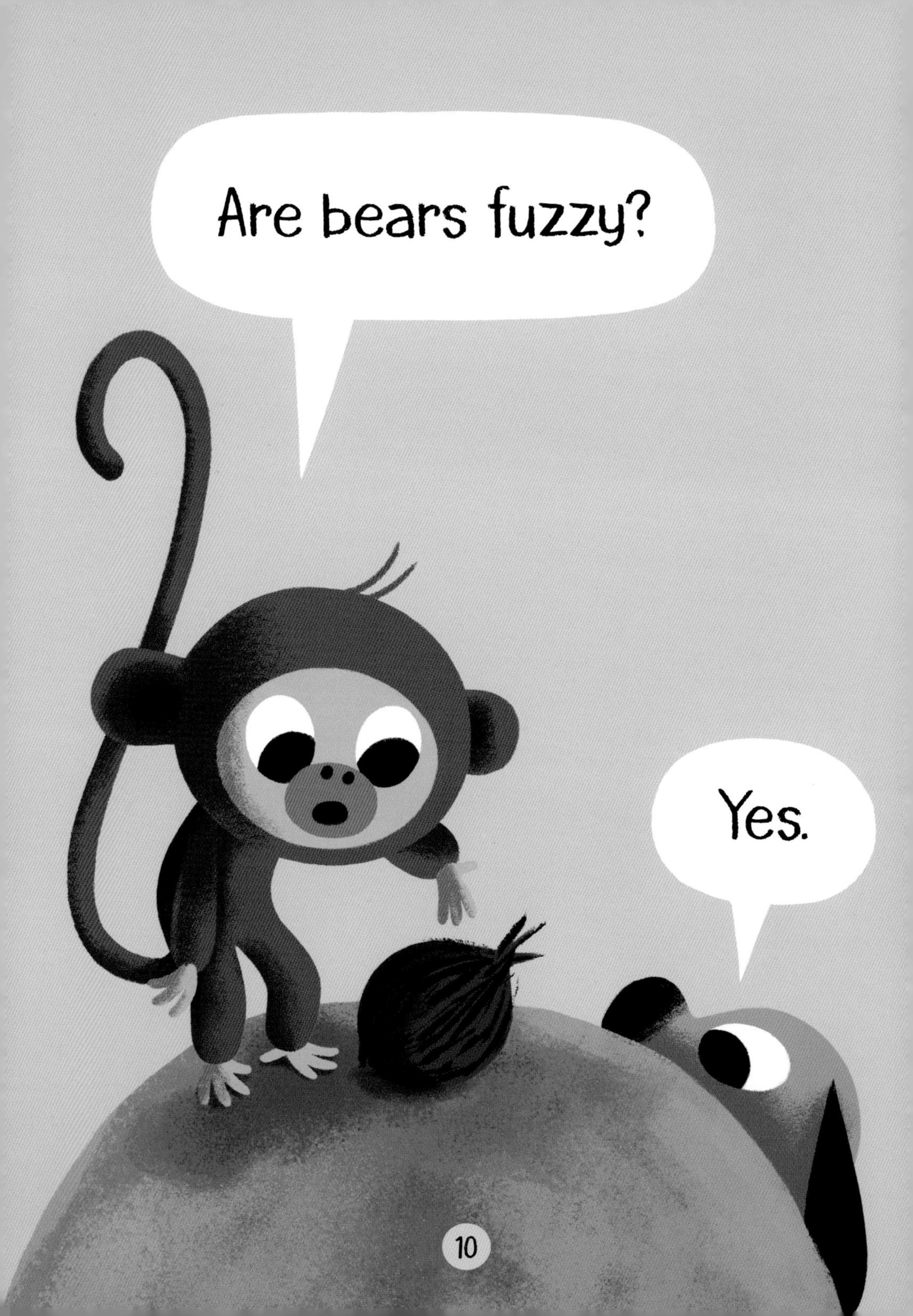
Are bears fuzzy?
Yes.

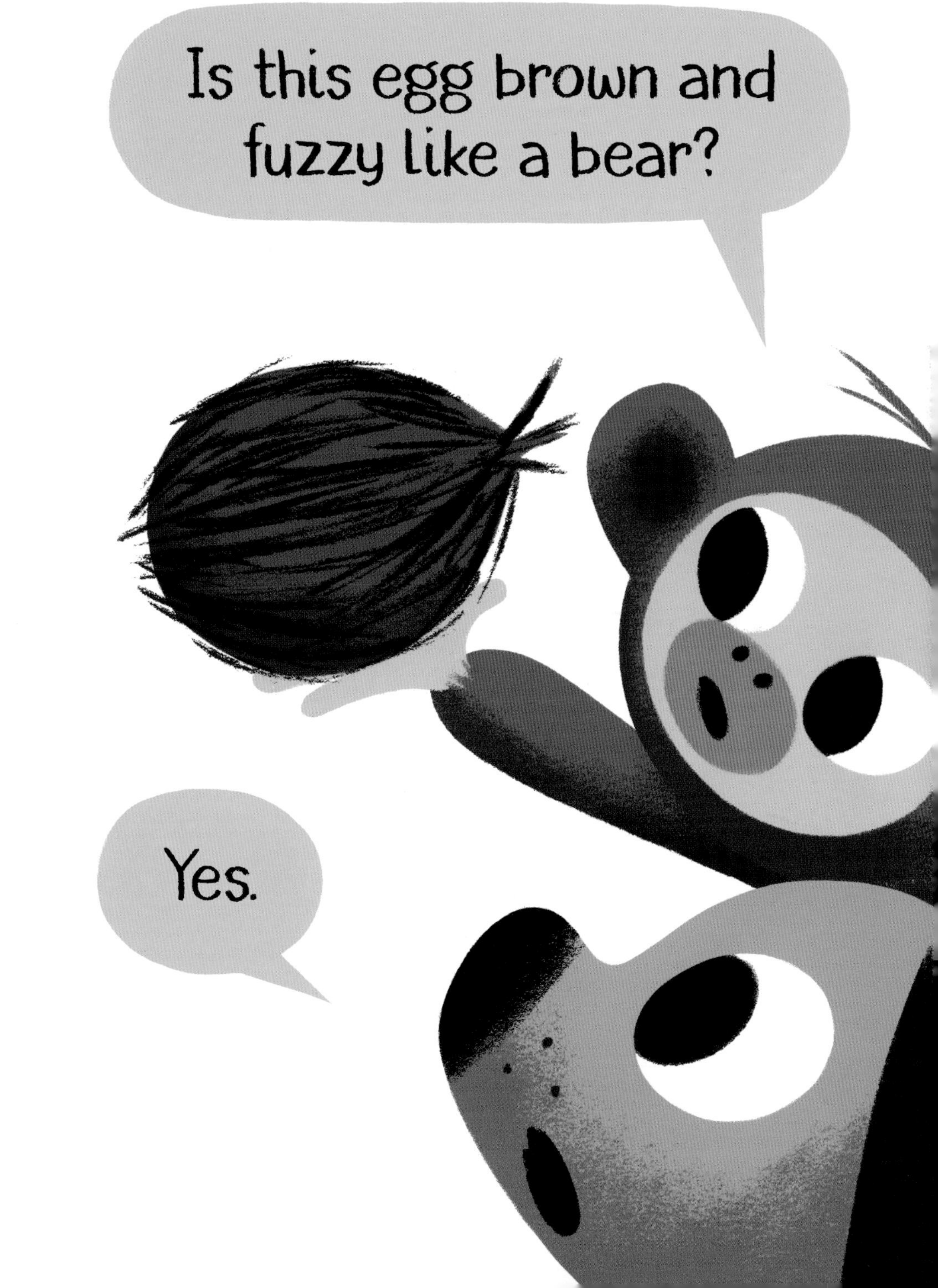
Is this egg brown and fuzzy like a bear?
Yes.

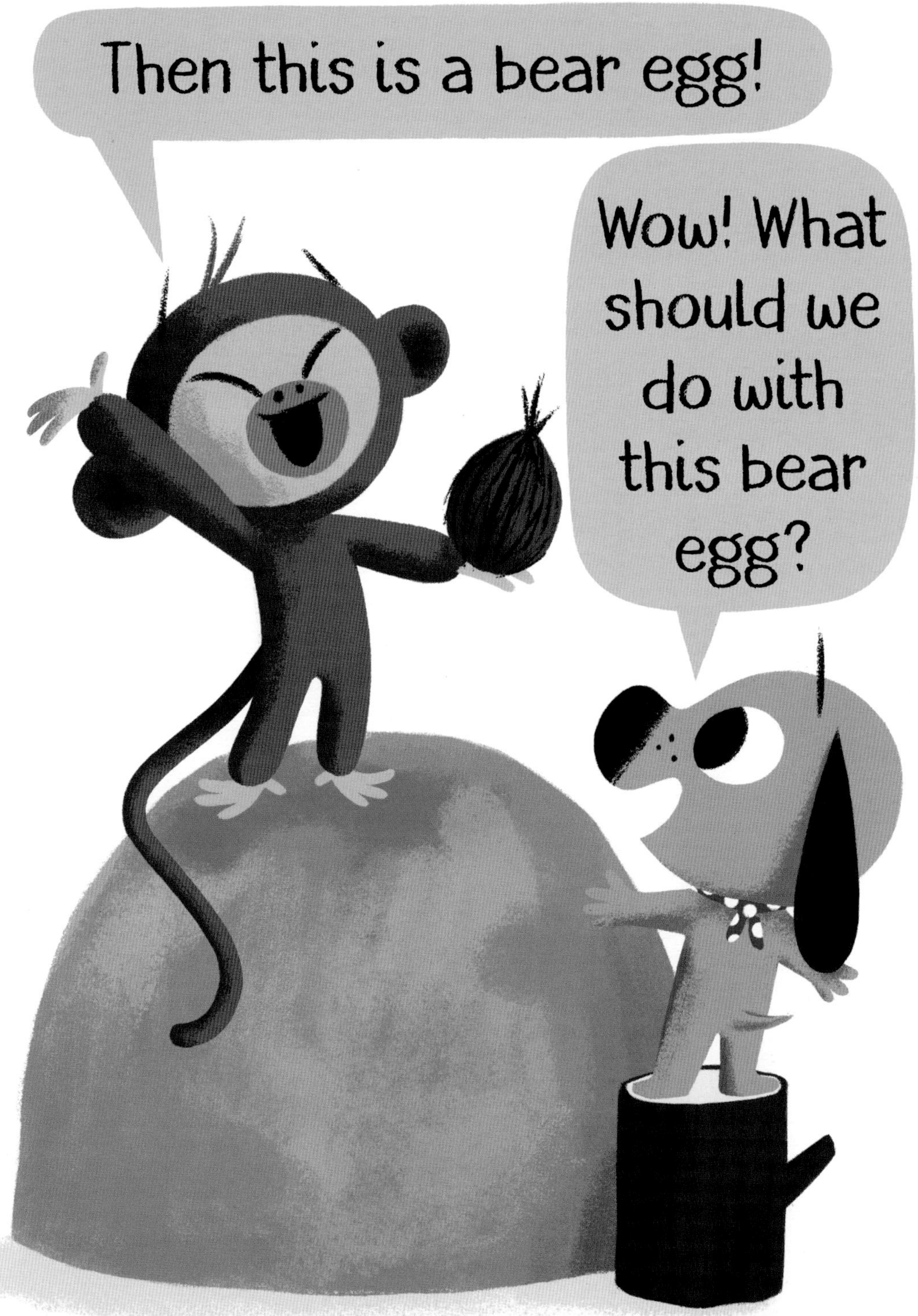
Then this is a bear egg!
Wow! What should we do with this bear egg?

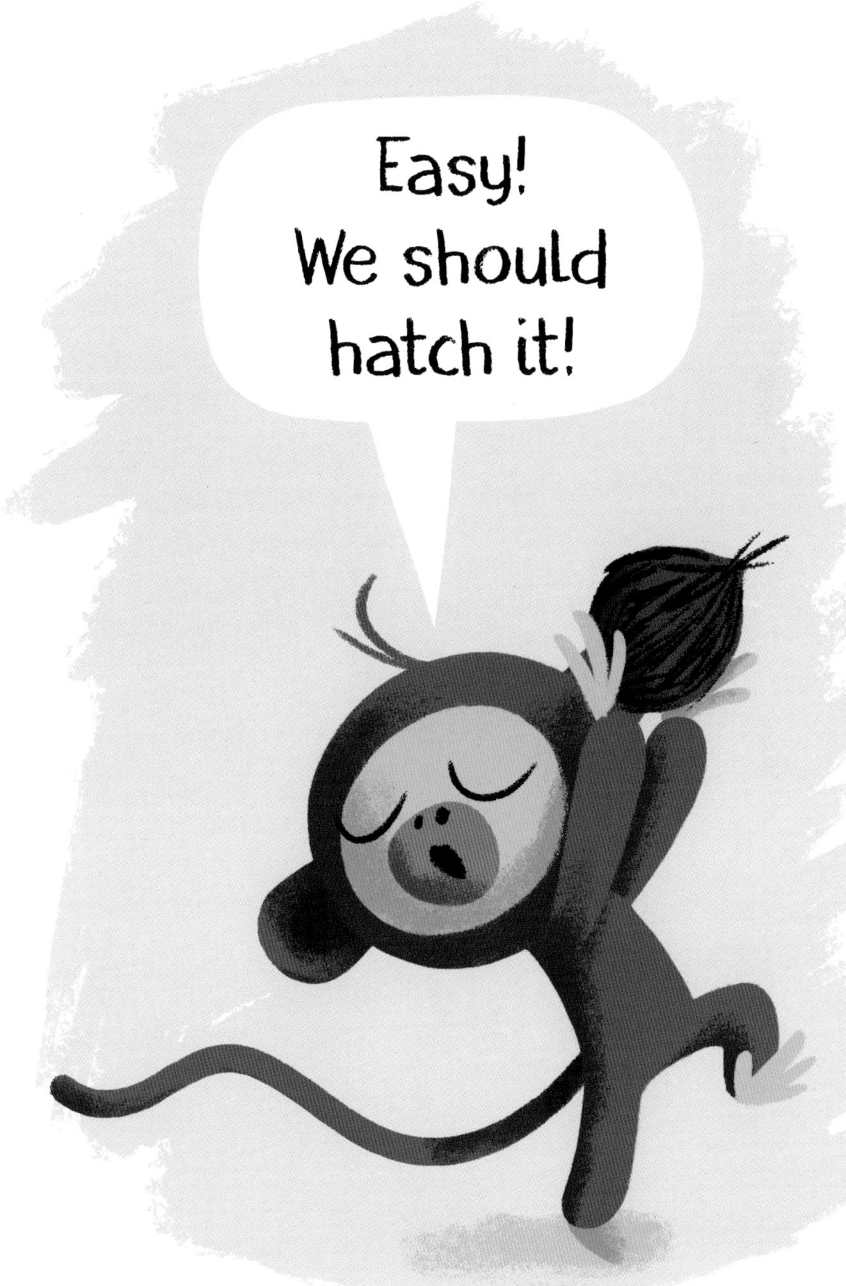
Easy! We should hatch it!

Chapter 2
Egg Hatching for Beginners

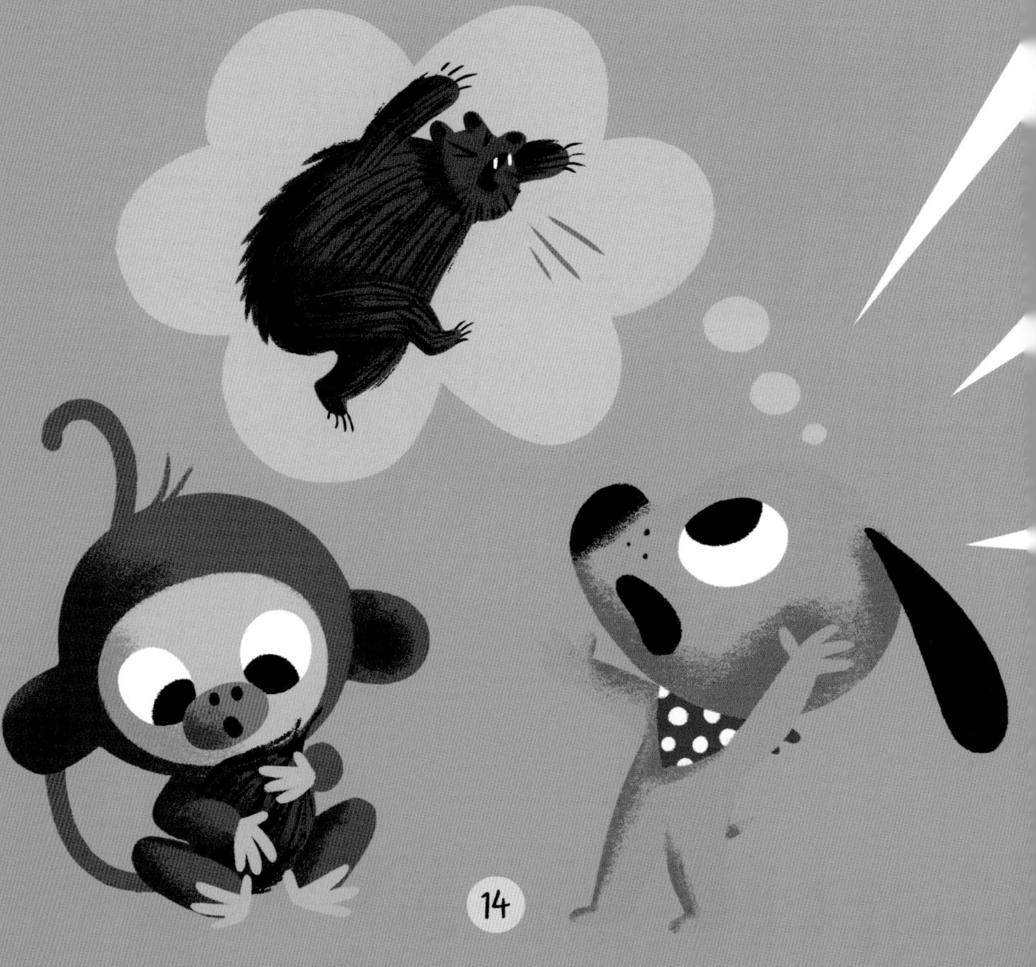

HATCH THE EGG?

What if a big bear
hatches from the egg . . .

and eats us???

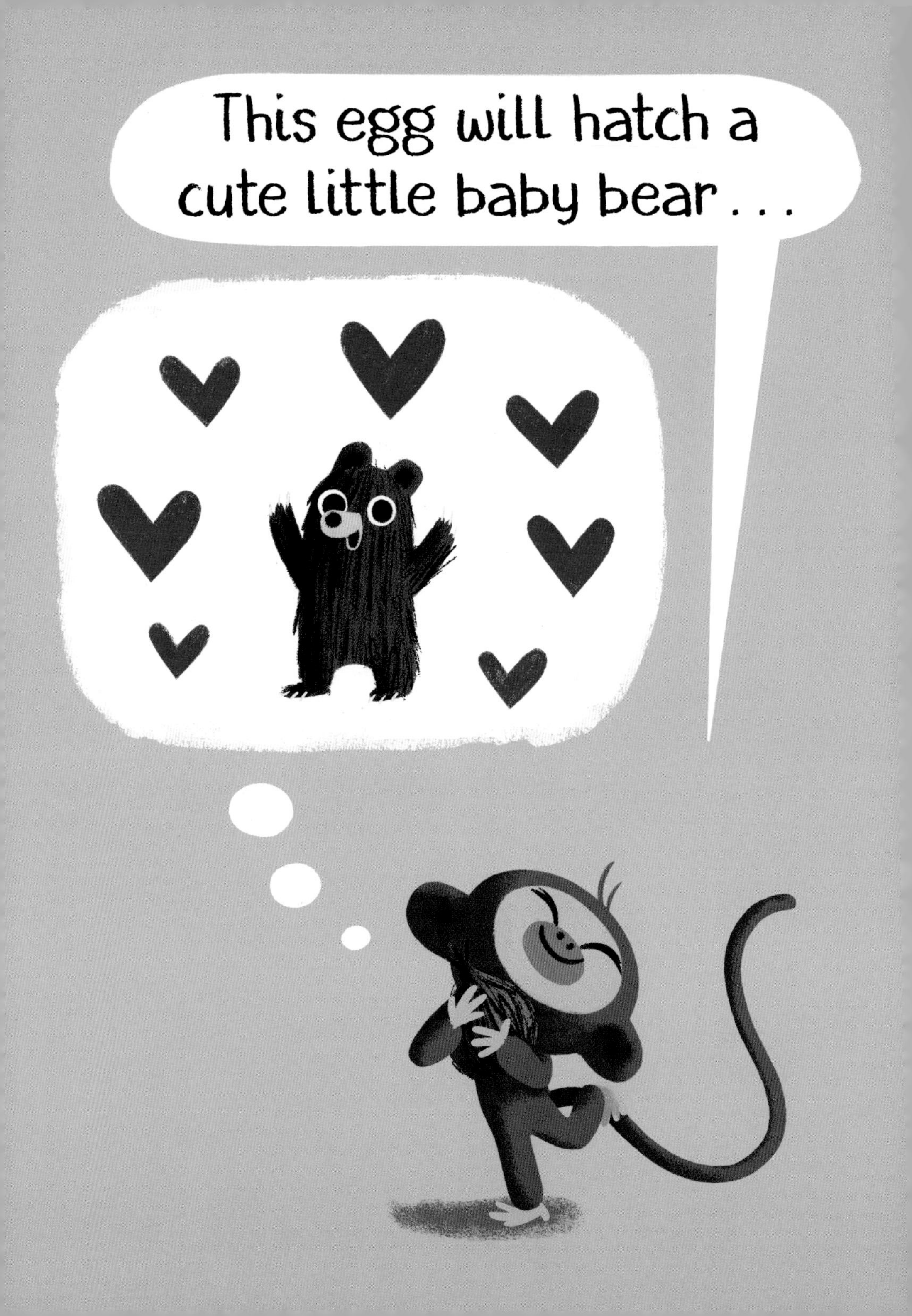
This egg will hatch a cute little baby bear . . .

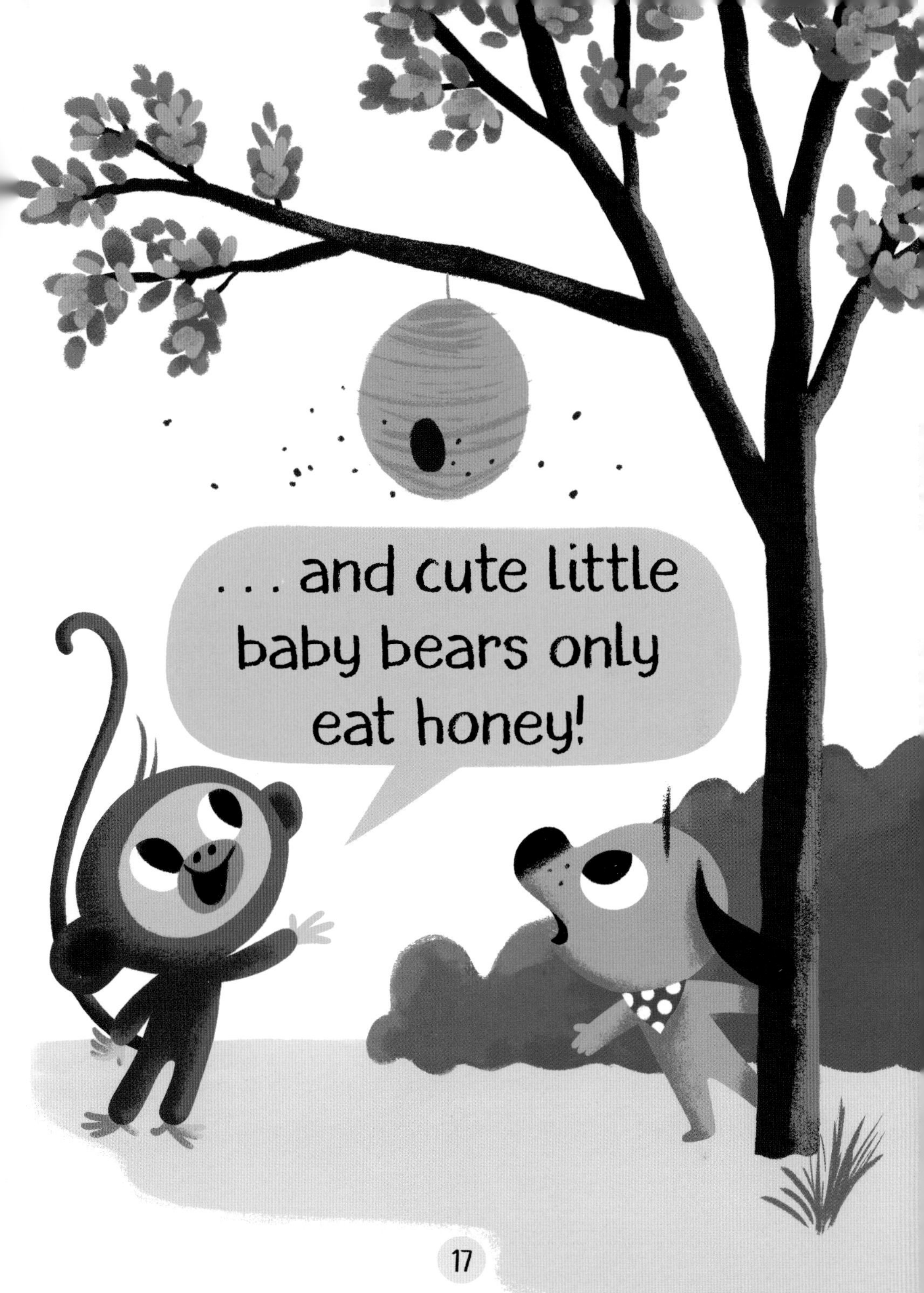
. . . and cute little
baby bears only
eat honey!

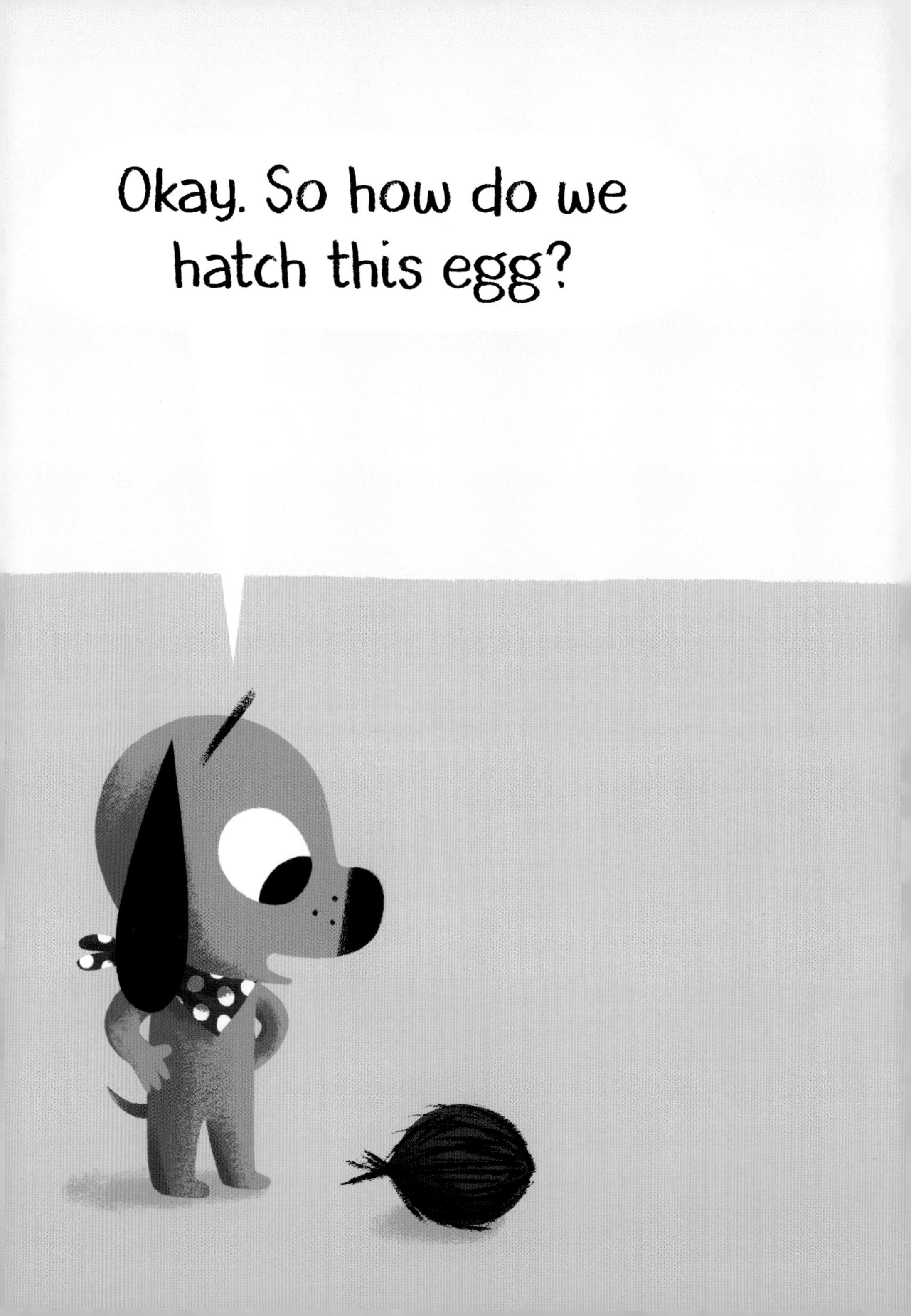
Okay. So how do we hatch this egg?

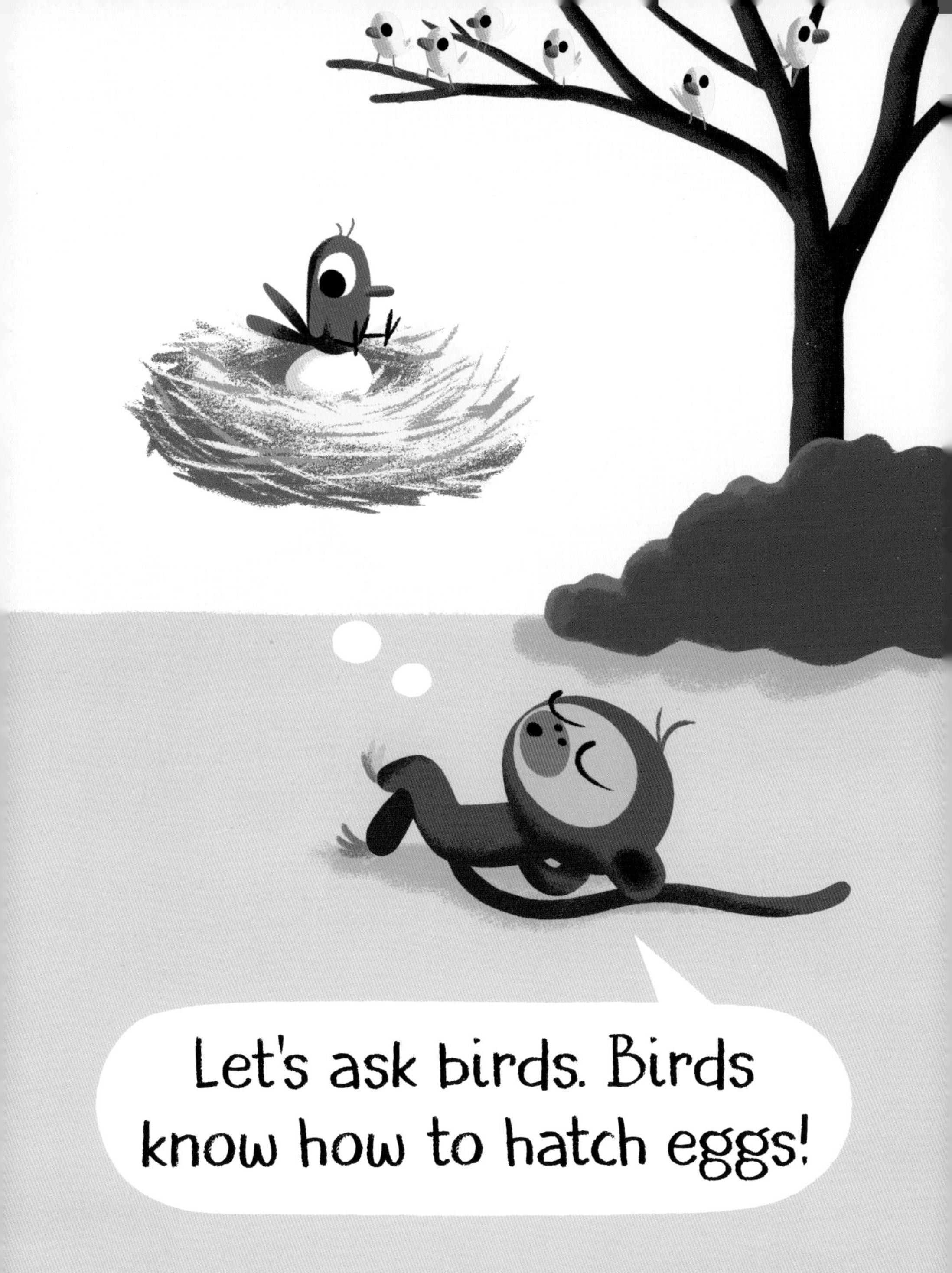
Let's ask birds. Birds know how to hatch eggs!

Chapter 3

The Big Nest

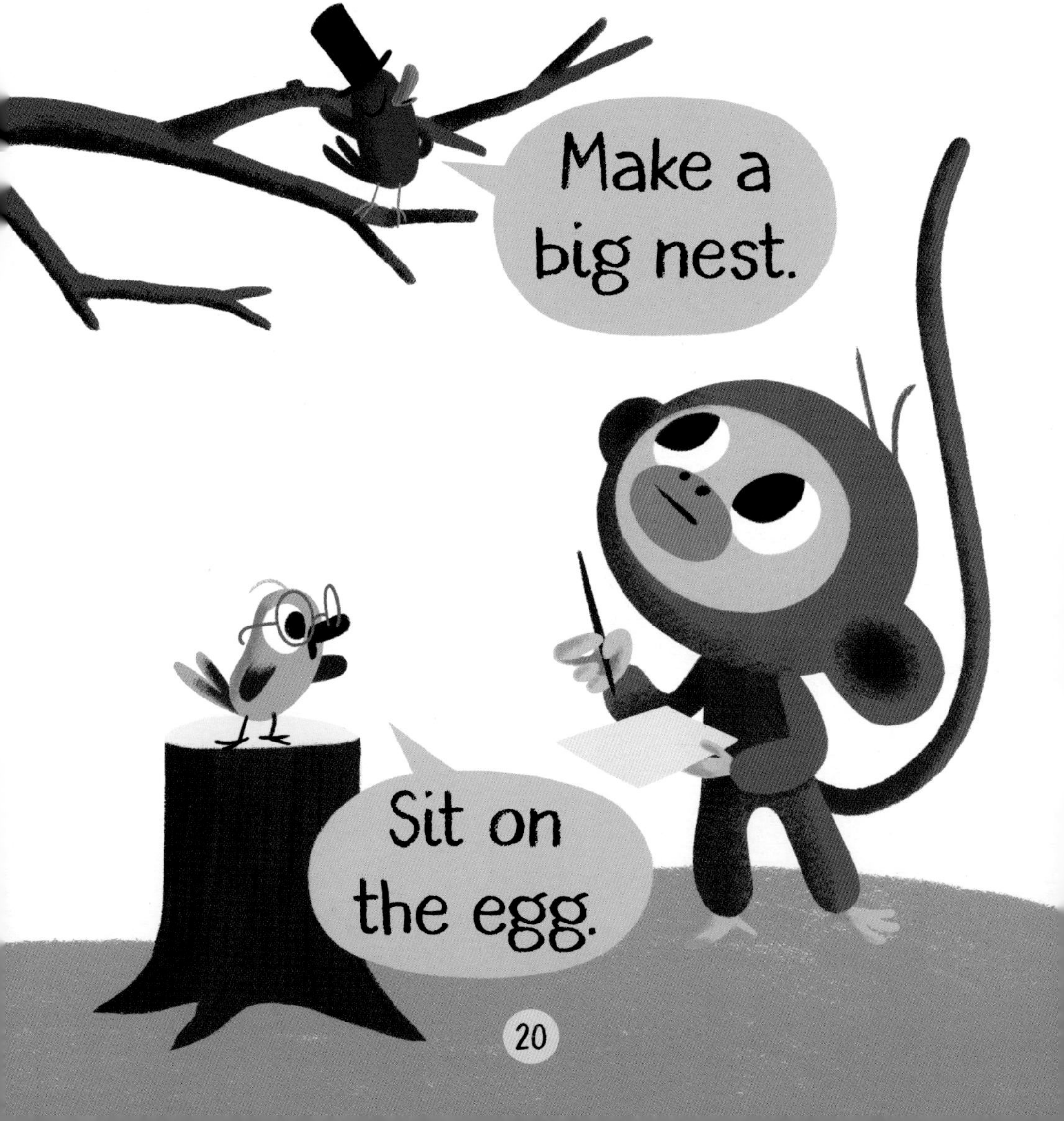

Make a big nest.
Sit on the egg.

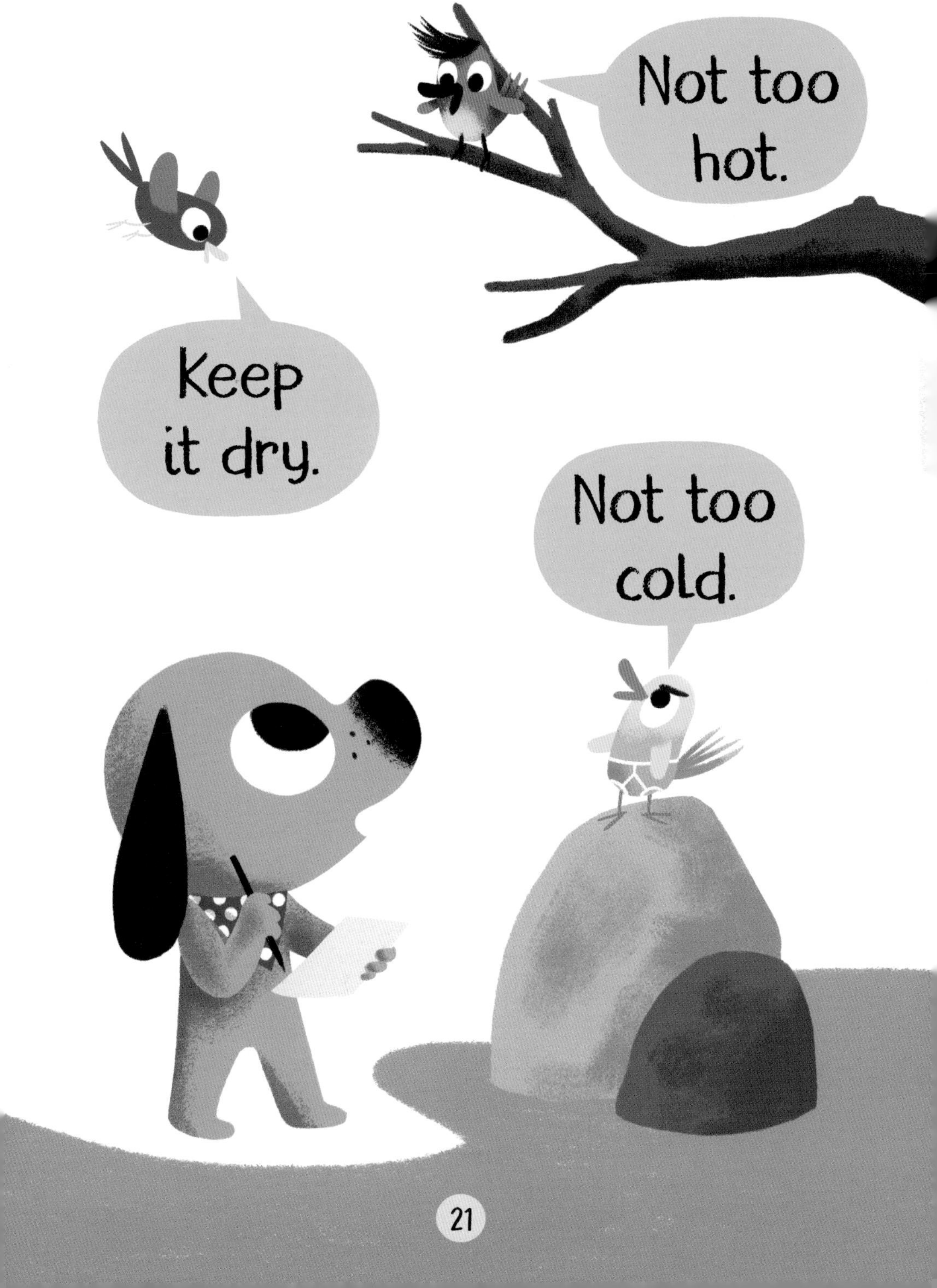
Not too hot.
Keep it dry.
Not too cold.

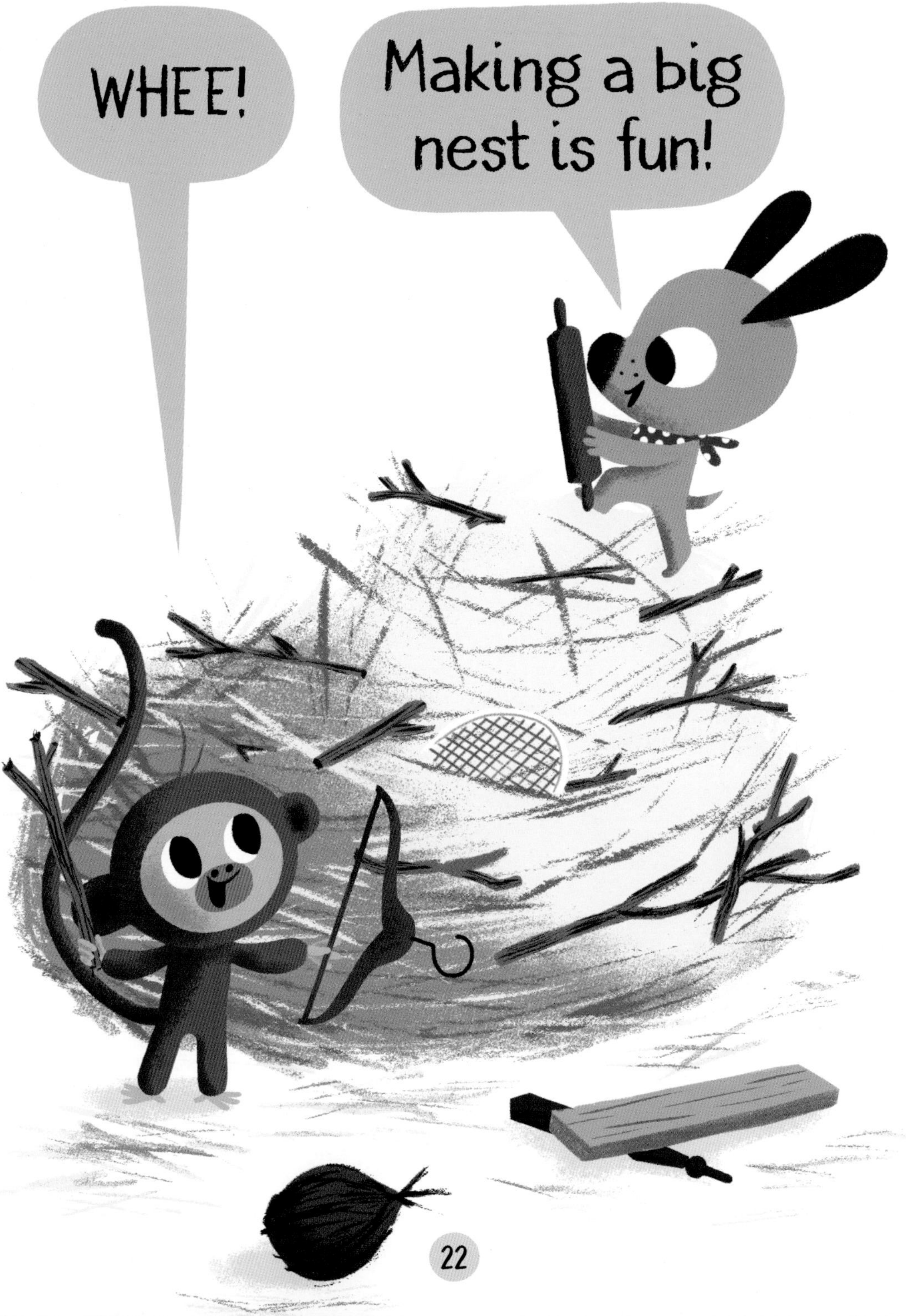
WHEE!
Making a big nest is fun!

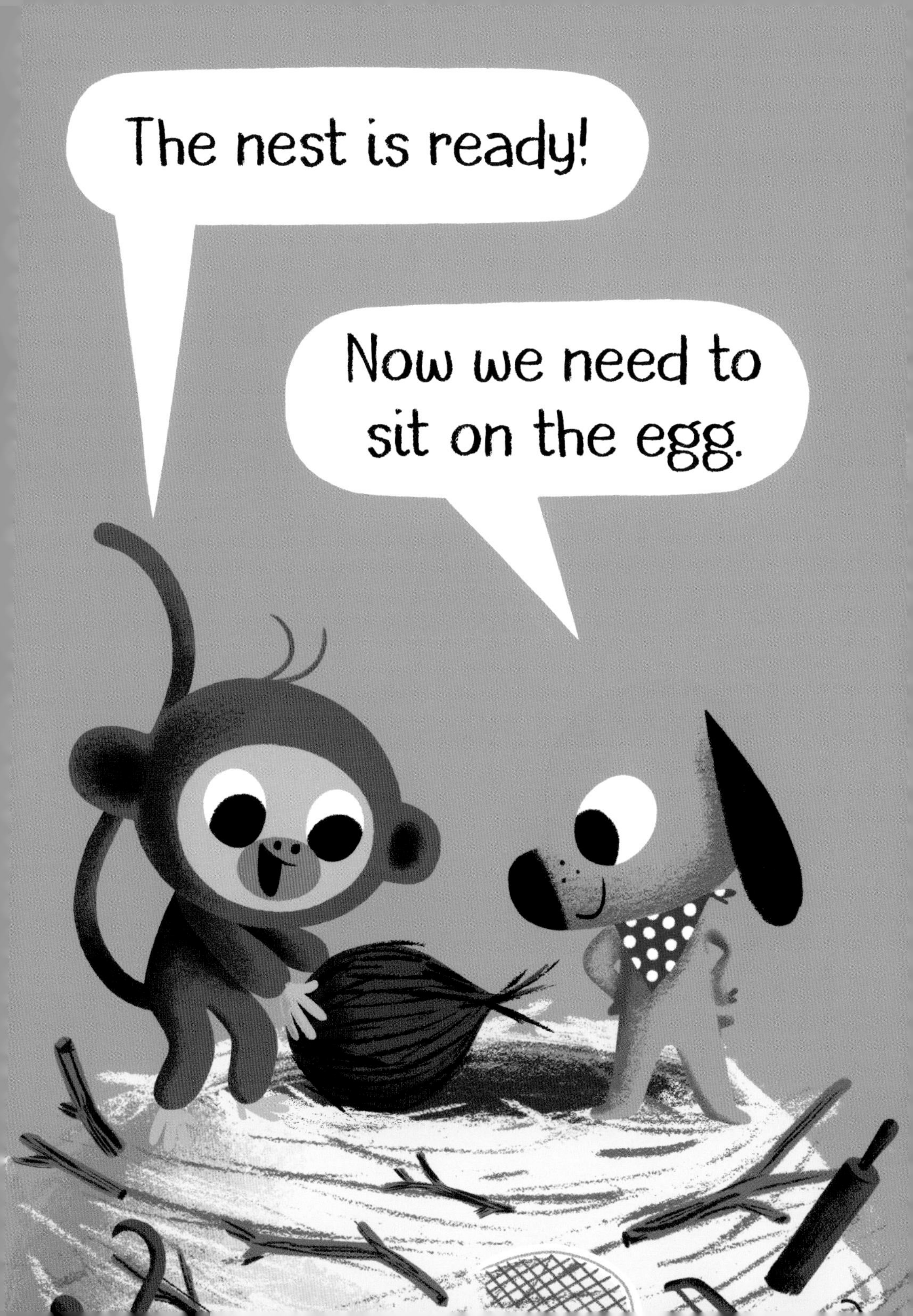
The nest is ready!
Now we need to sit on the egg.

Chapter 4
The Long Wait

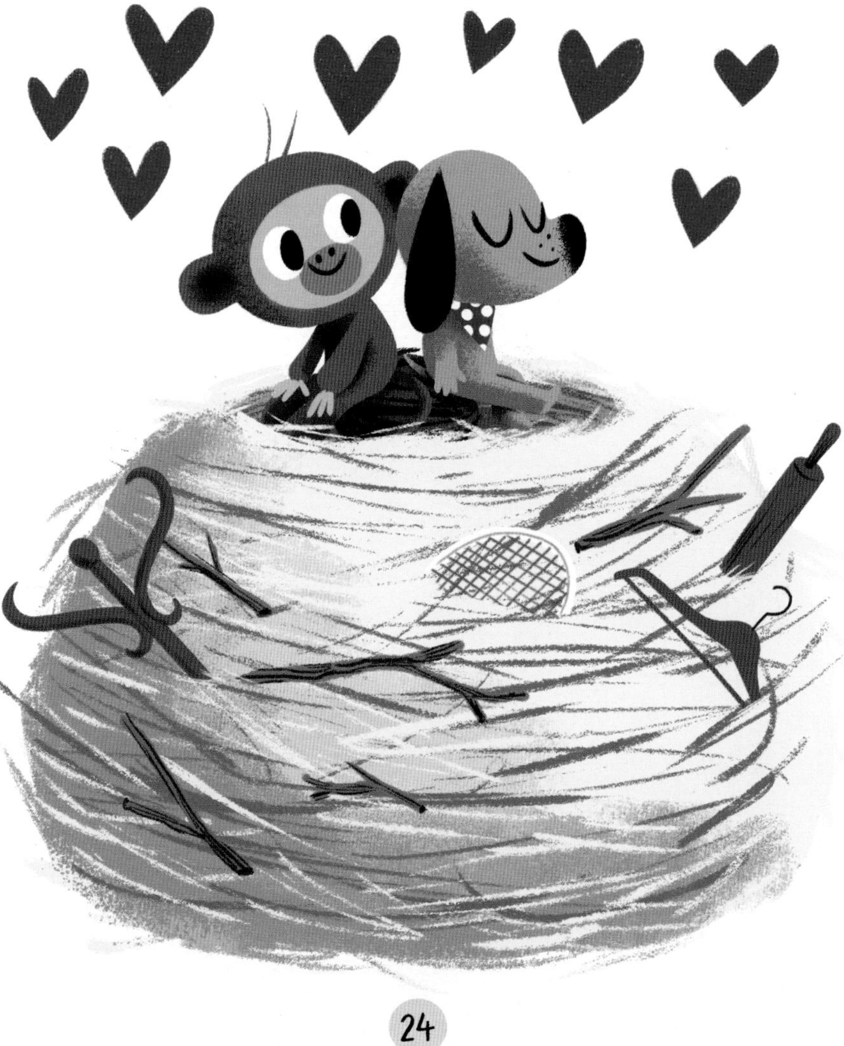

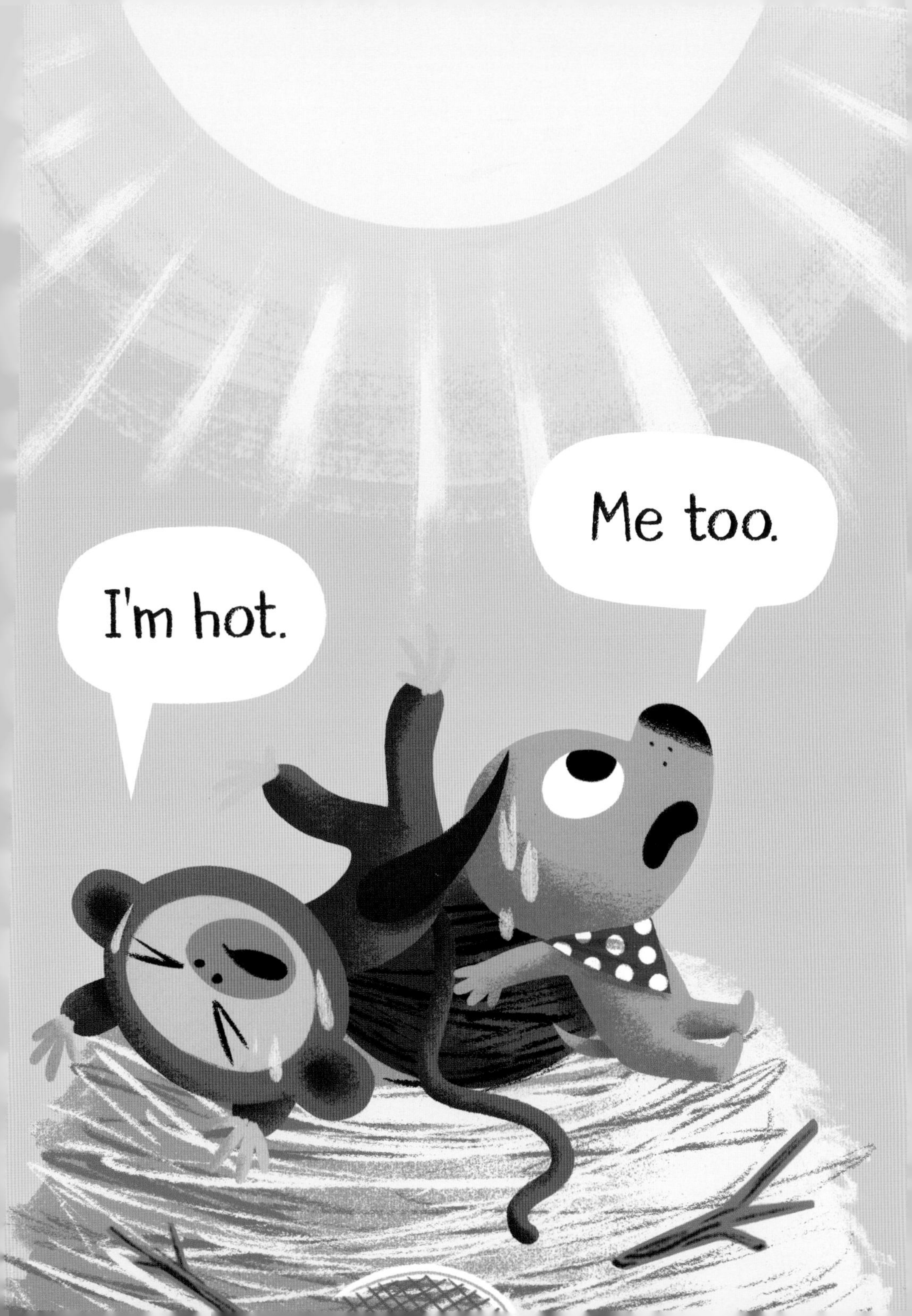
I'm hot.
Me too.

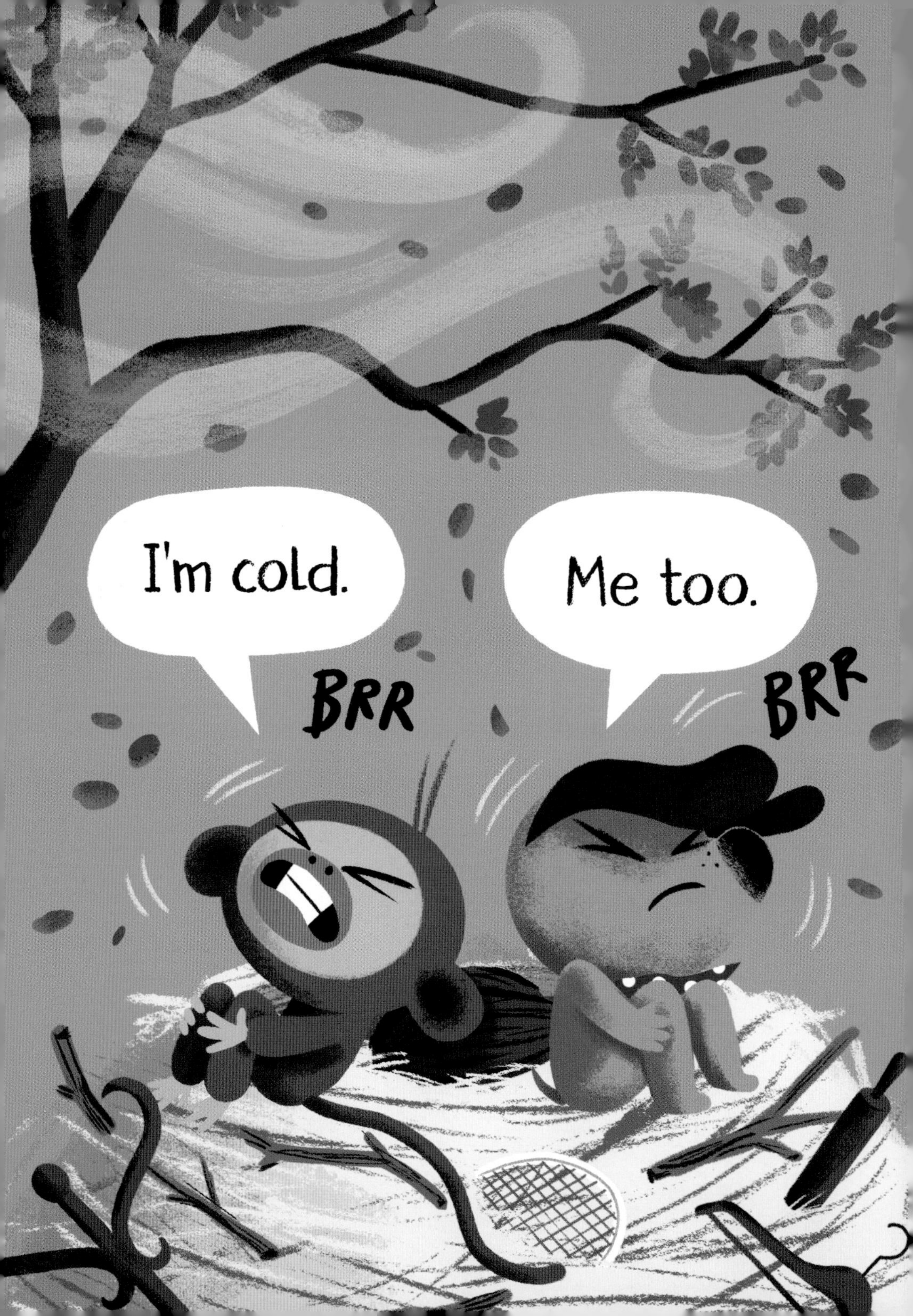
I'm cold.
BRR
Me too.
BRR

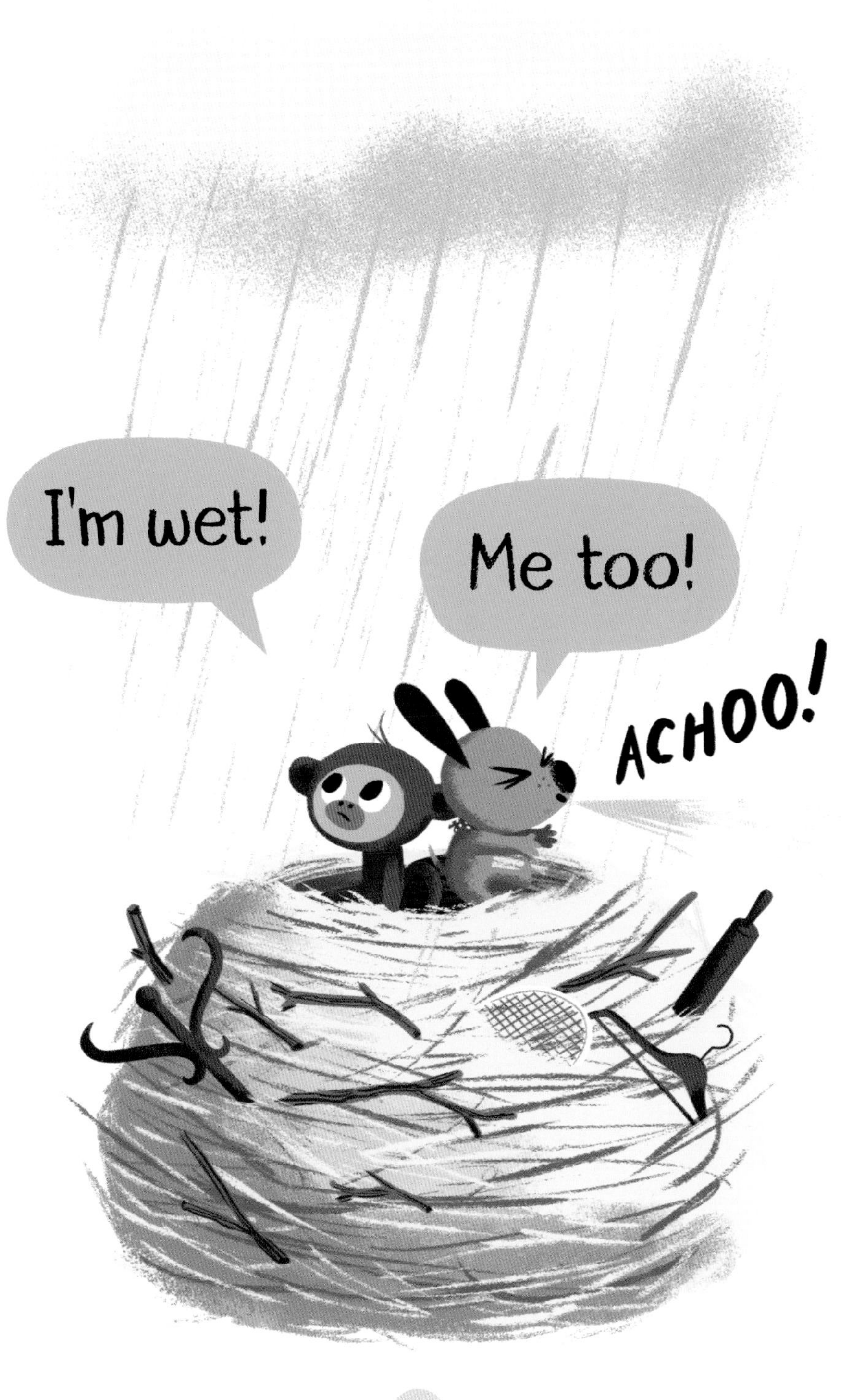
I'm wet!
Me too!
ACHOO!

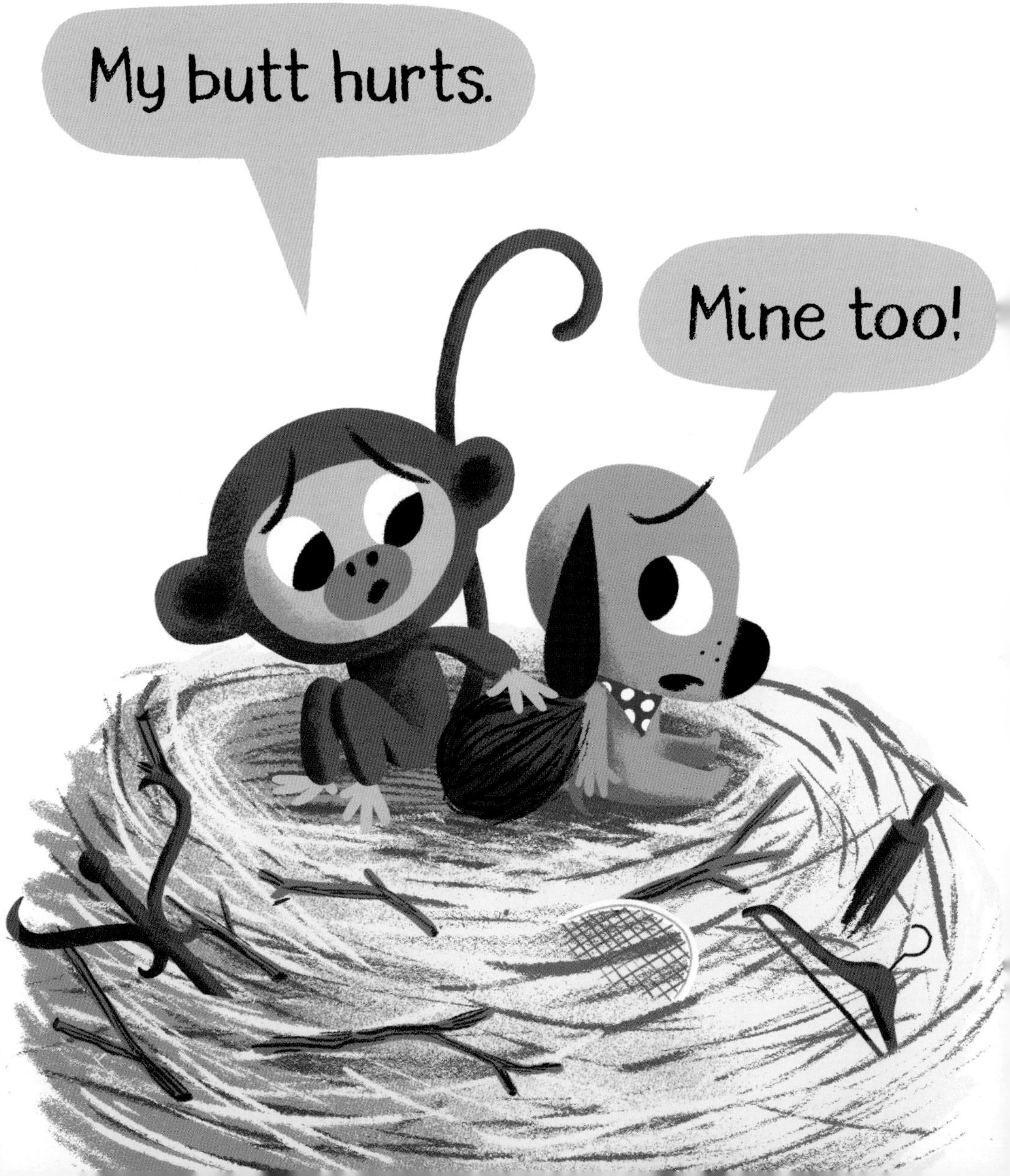
My butt hurts.
Mine too!

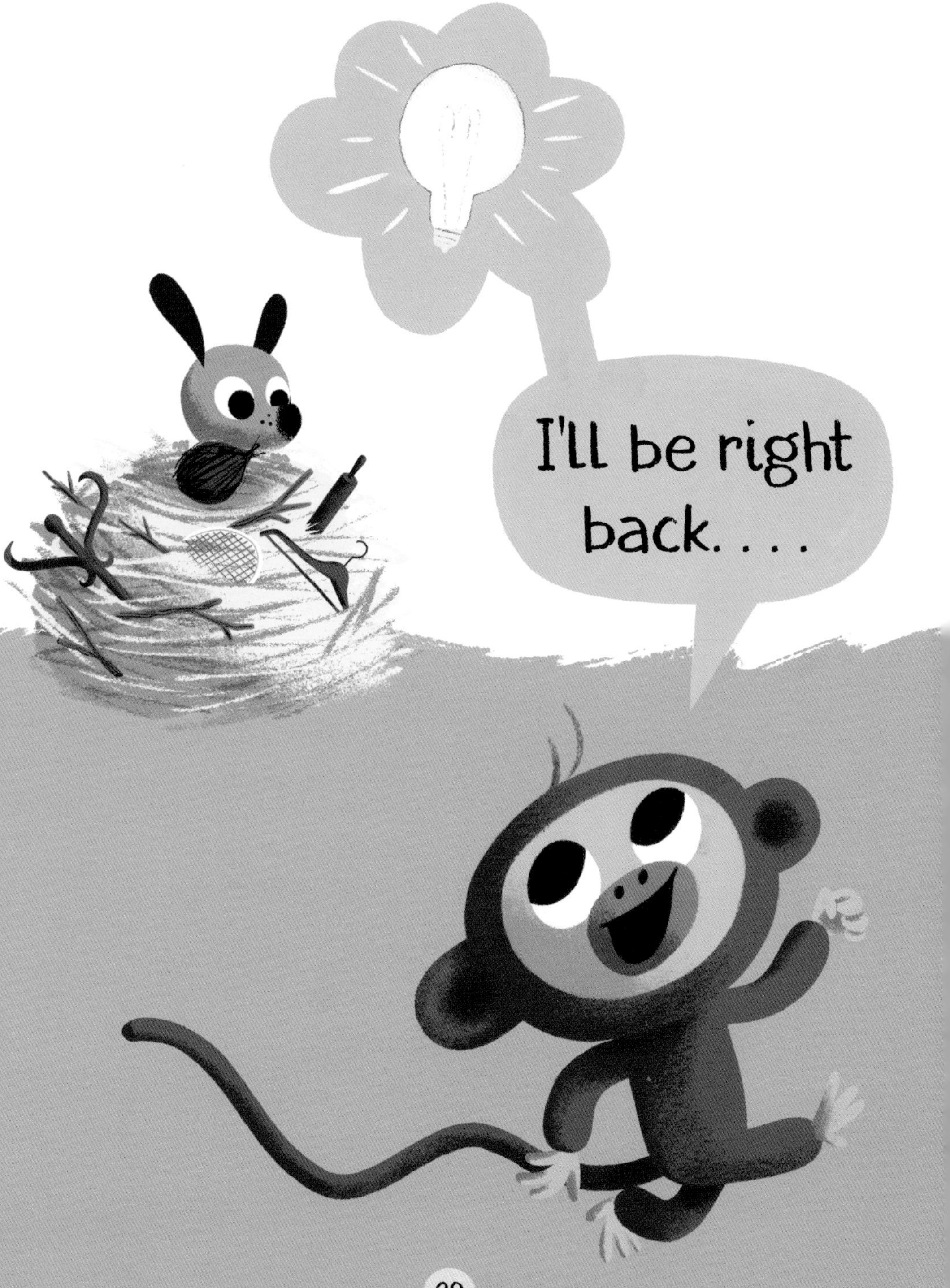
I'll be right back. . . .

Chapter 5
The Smell of Honey

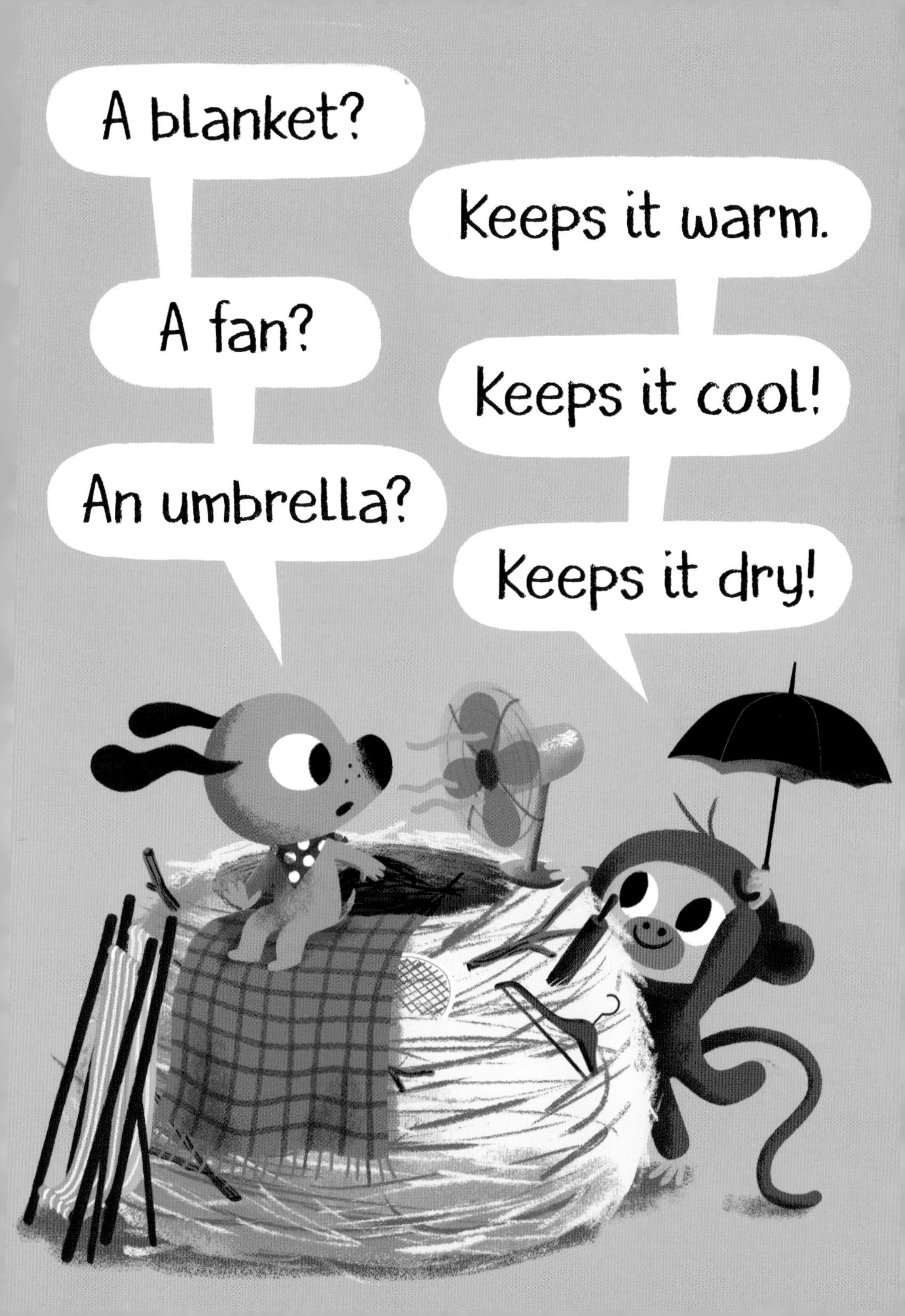
A blanket?
Keeps it warm.
A fan?
Keeps it cool!
An umbrella?
Keeps it dry!

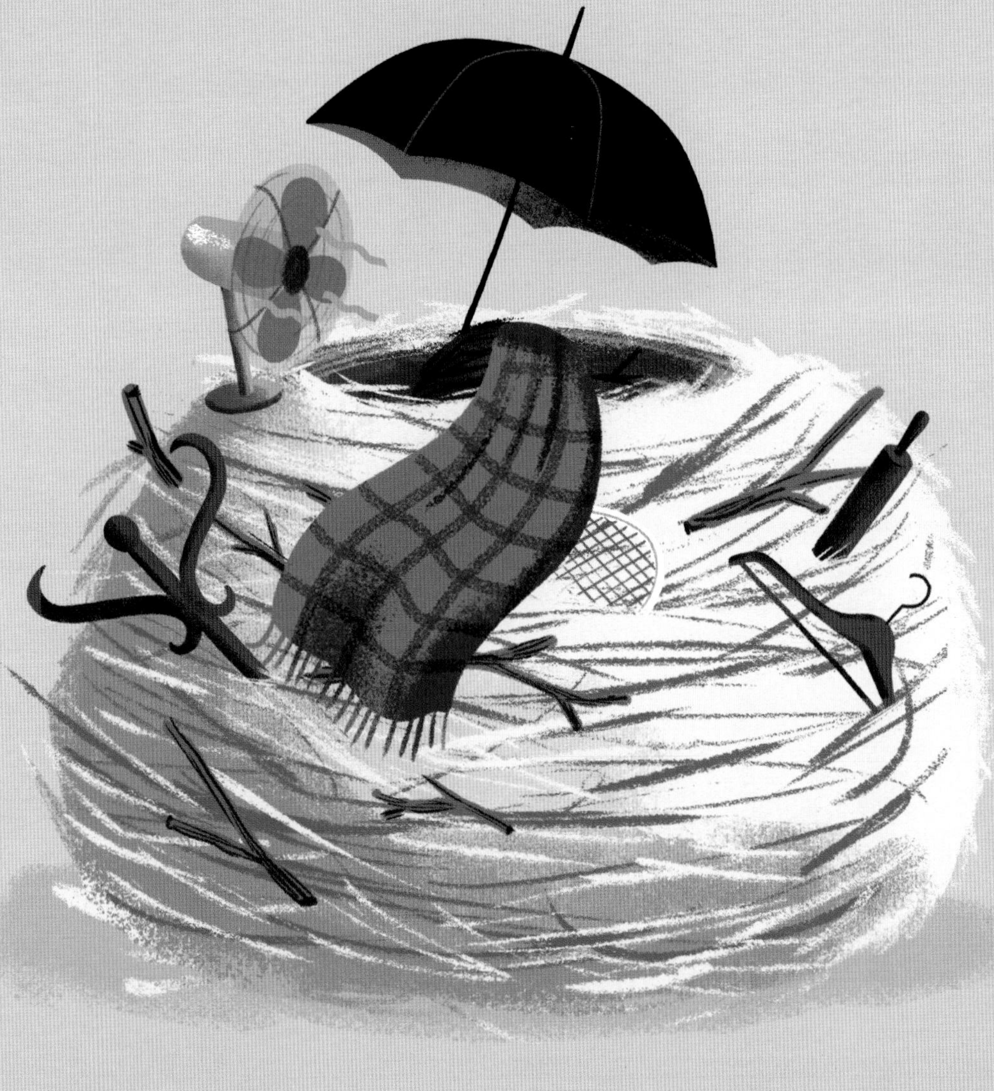

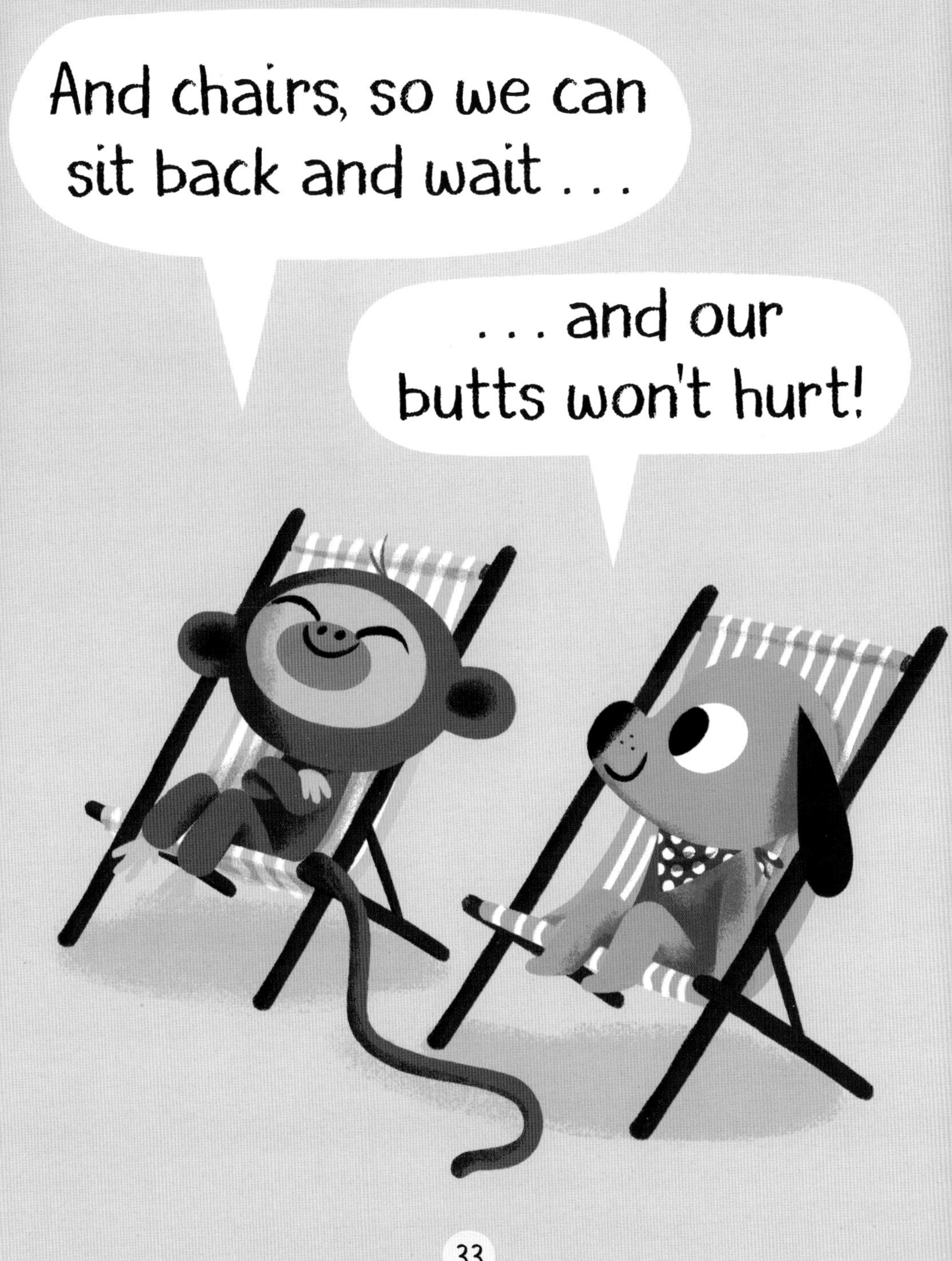
And chairs, so we can sit back and wait . . .
. . . and our butts won't hurt!

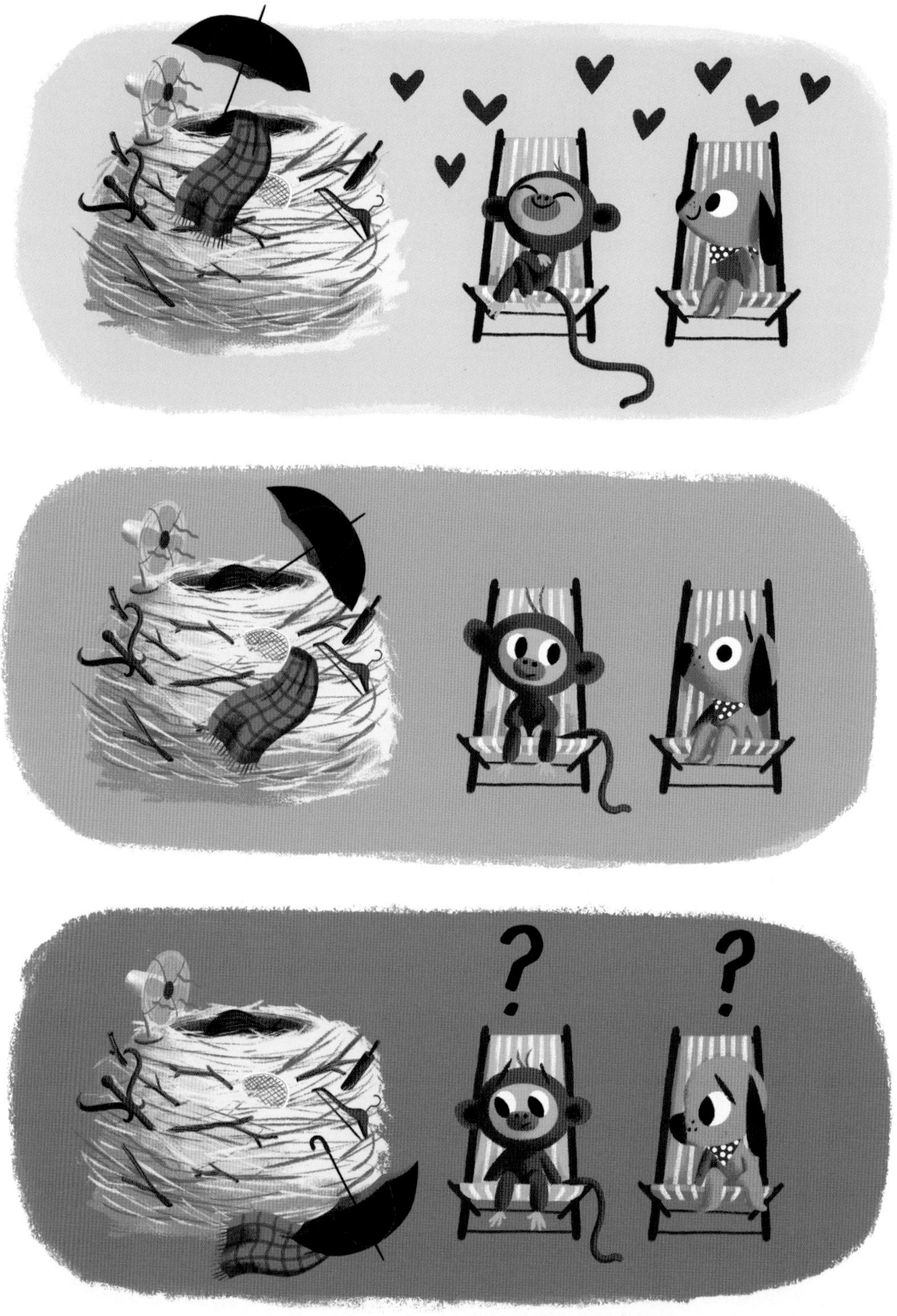

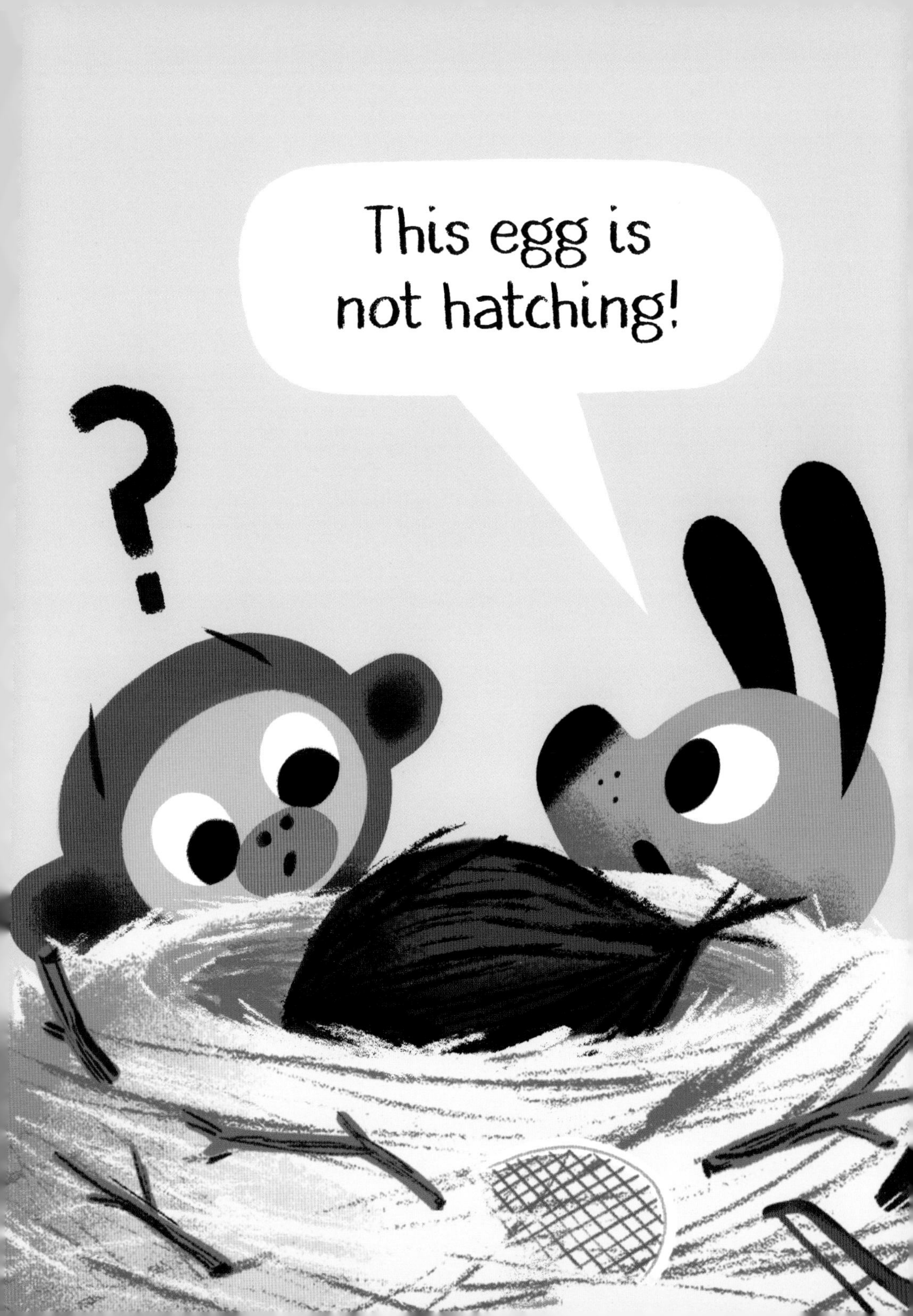
This egg is not hatching!
?

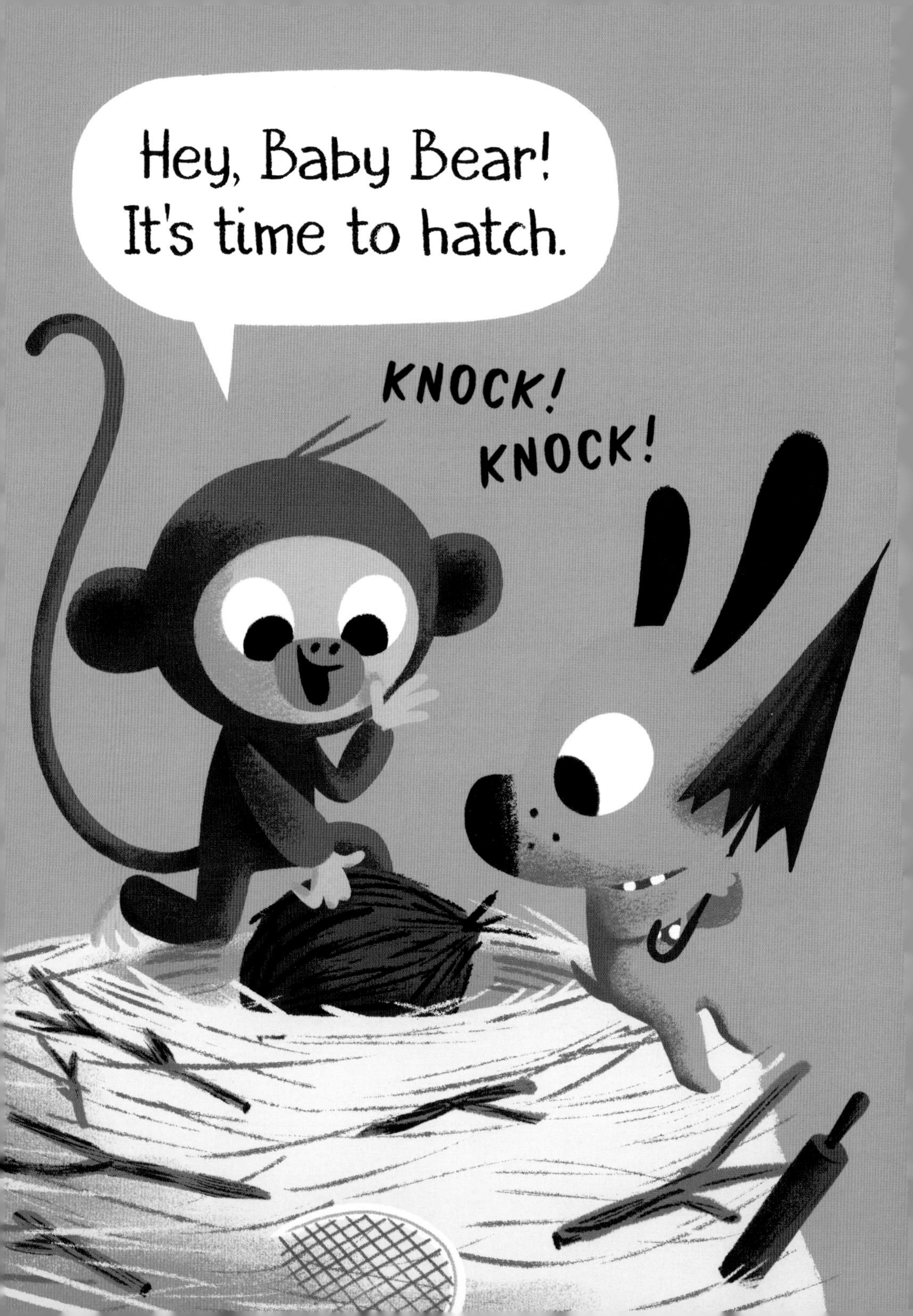
Hey, Baby Bear!
It's time to hatch.
KNOCK!
KNOCK!

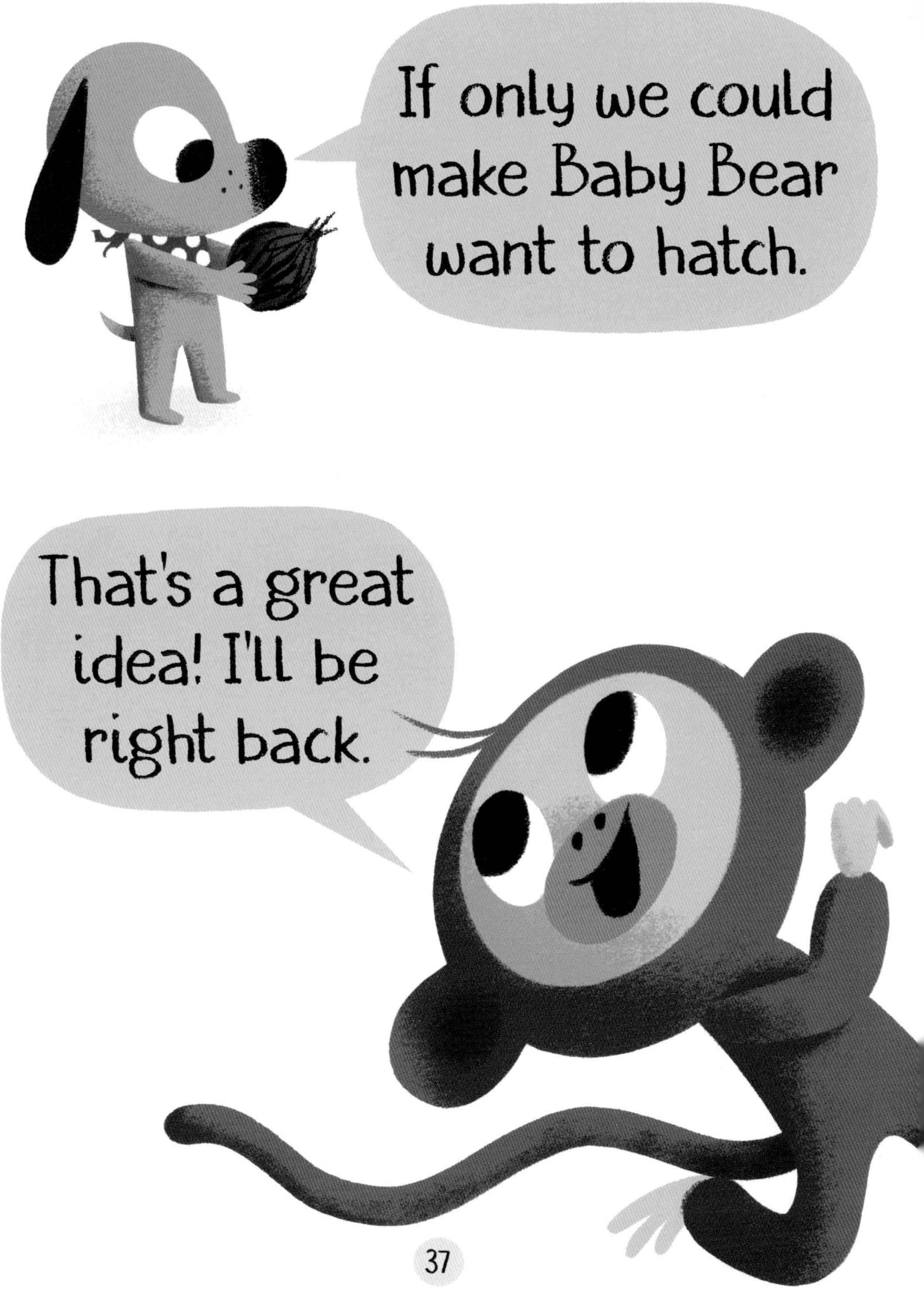
If only we could make Baby Bear want to hatch.
That's a great idea! I'll be right back.

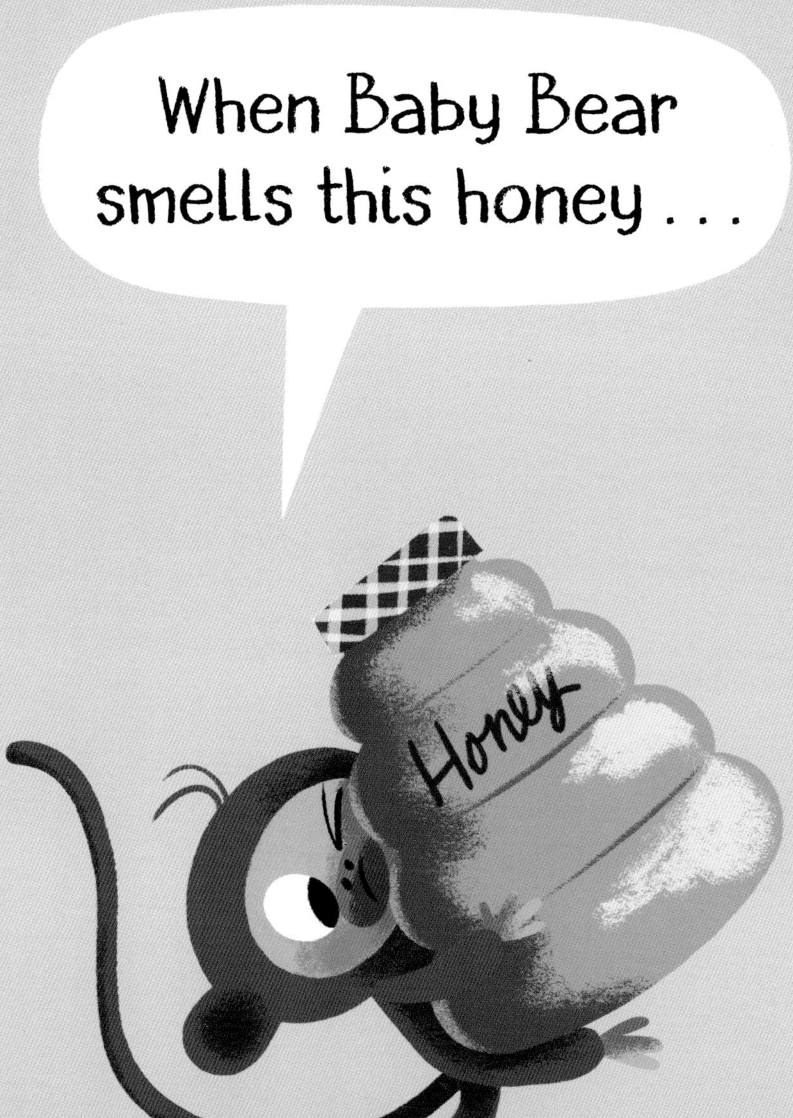
When Baby Bear smells this honey . . .
Honey

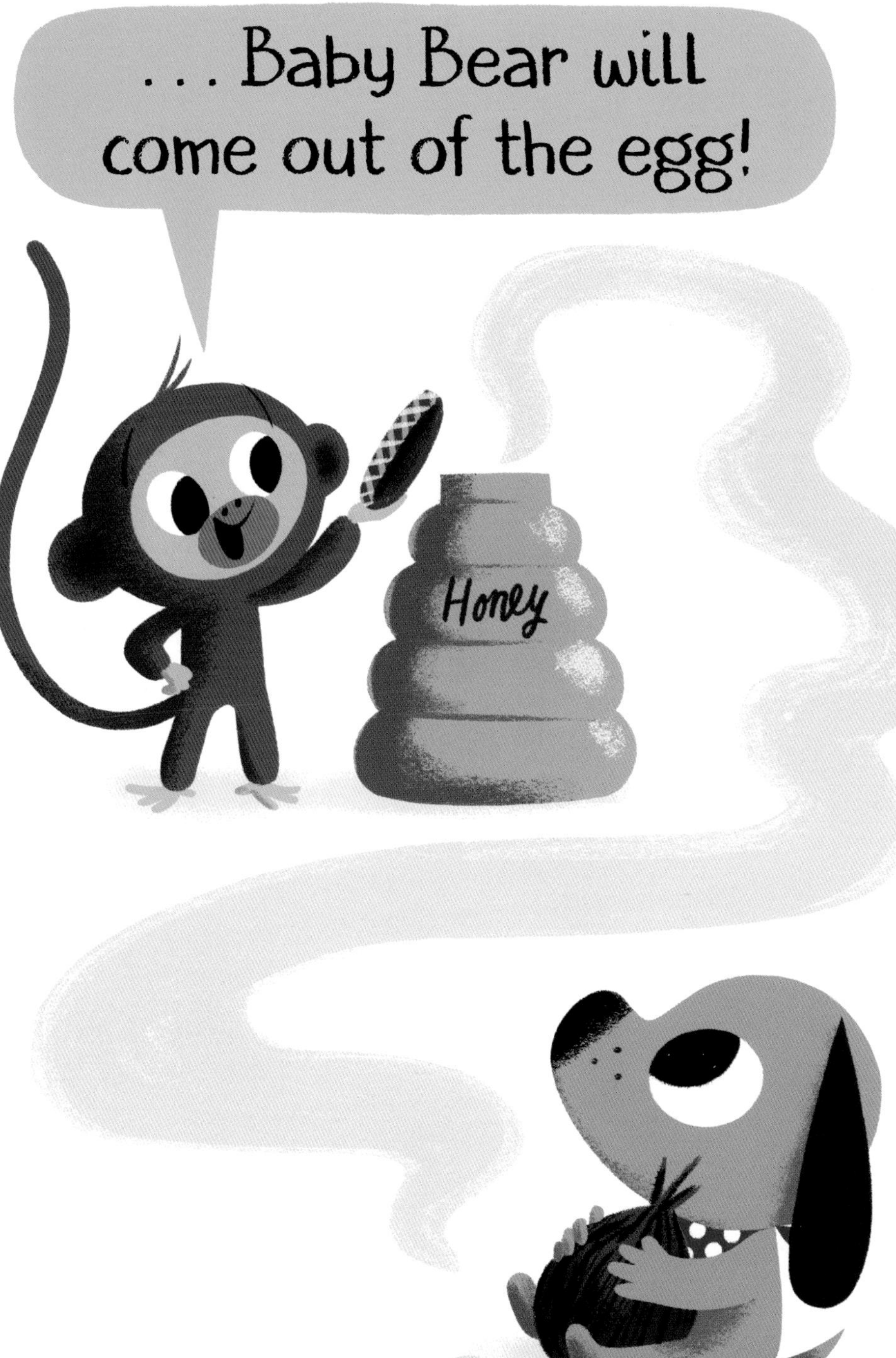
. . . Baby Bear will come out of the egg!
Honey

Chapter 6
The Hatching of Bears

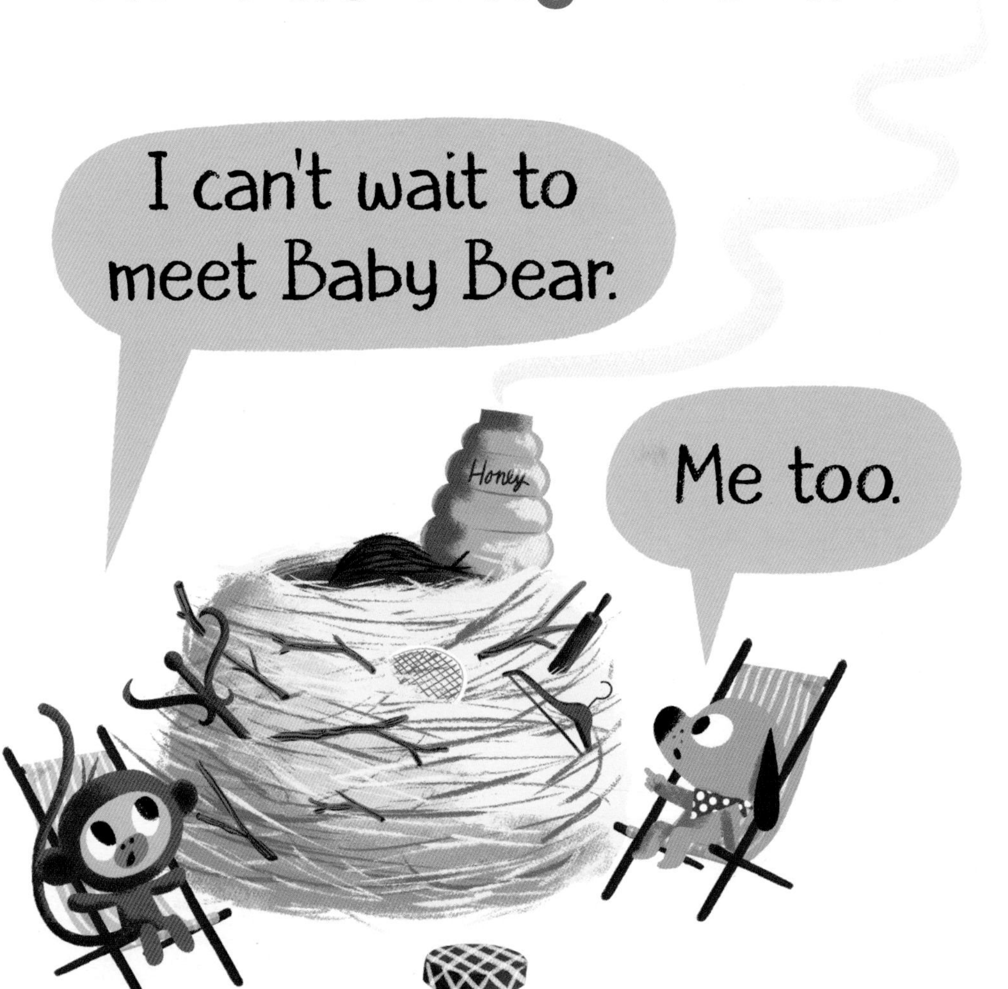
I can't wait to meet Baby Bear.
Honey
Me too.

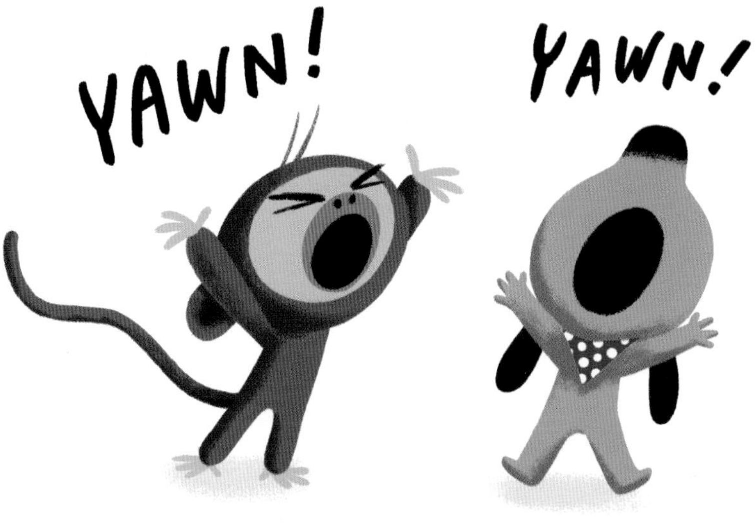
YAWN!
YAWN!

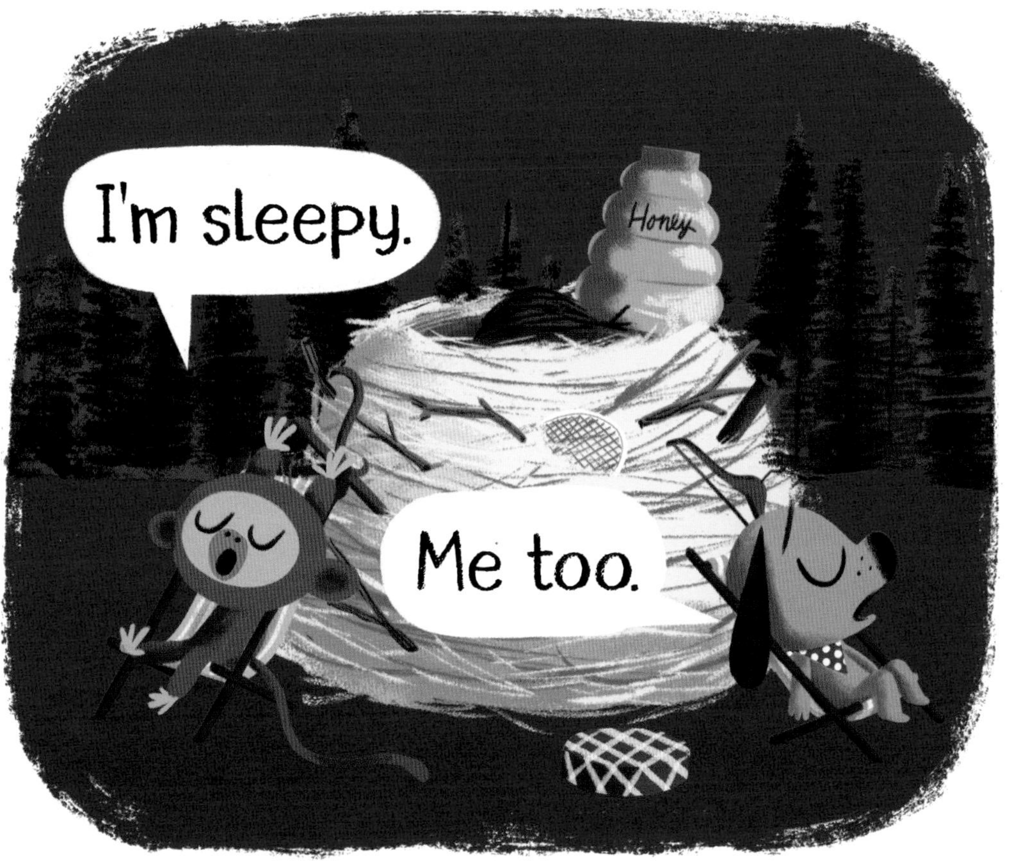
I'm sleepy.
Honey
Me too.

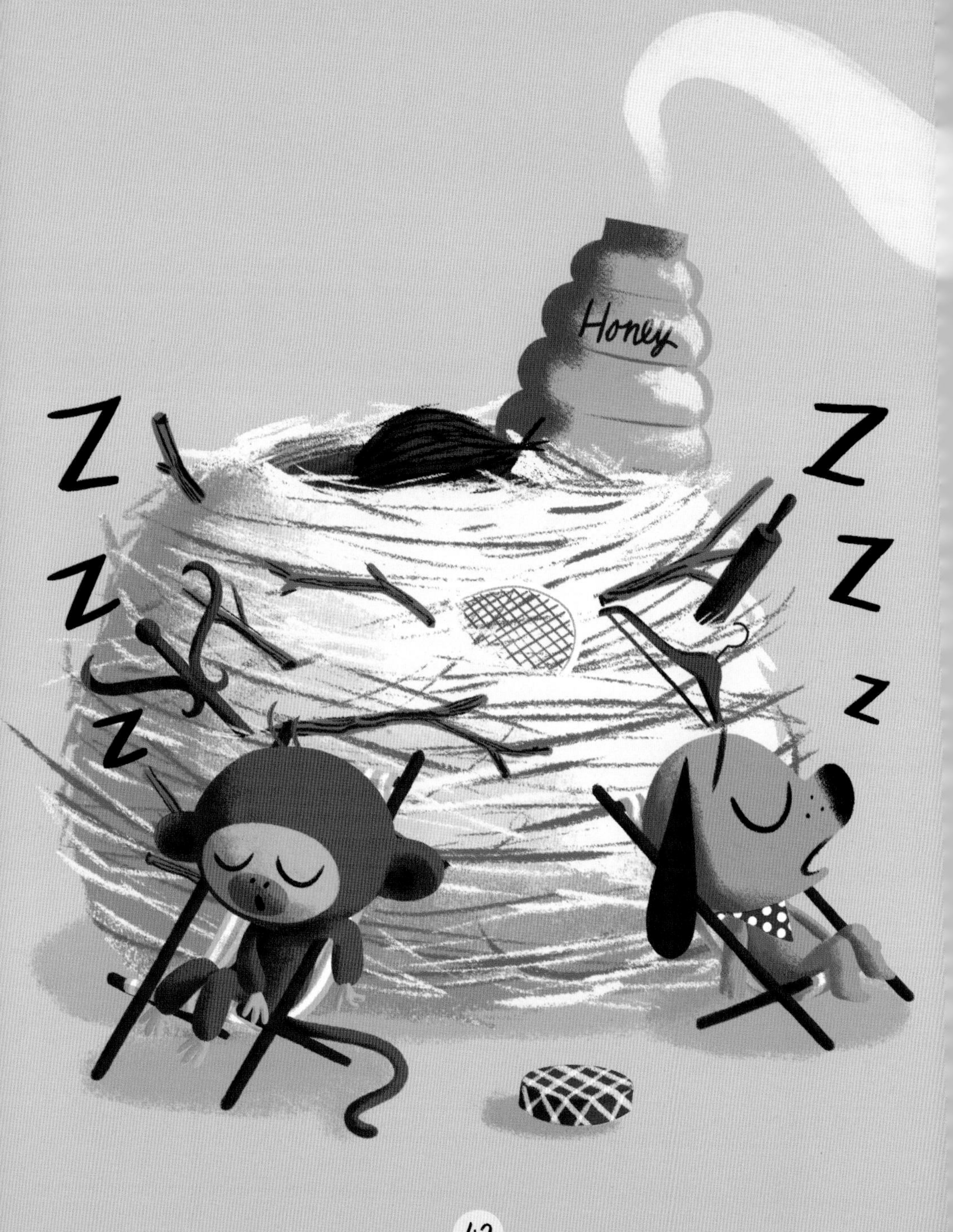
Honey
Z
Z
Z
Z
Z
Z
Z

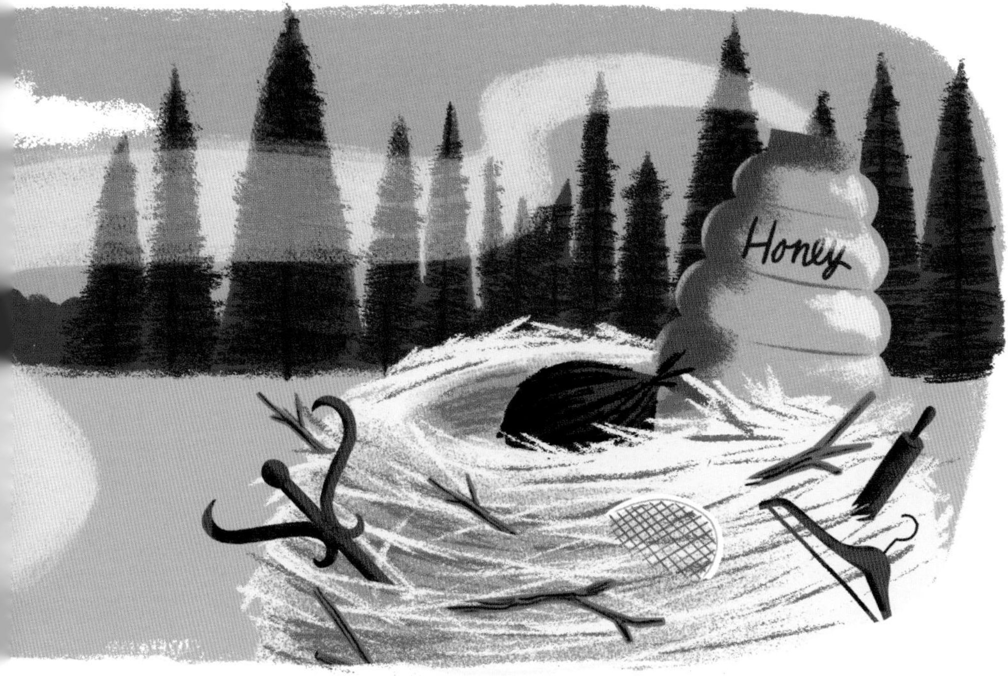
Honey

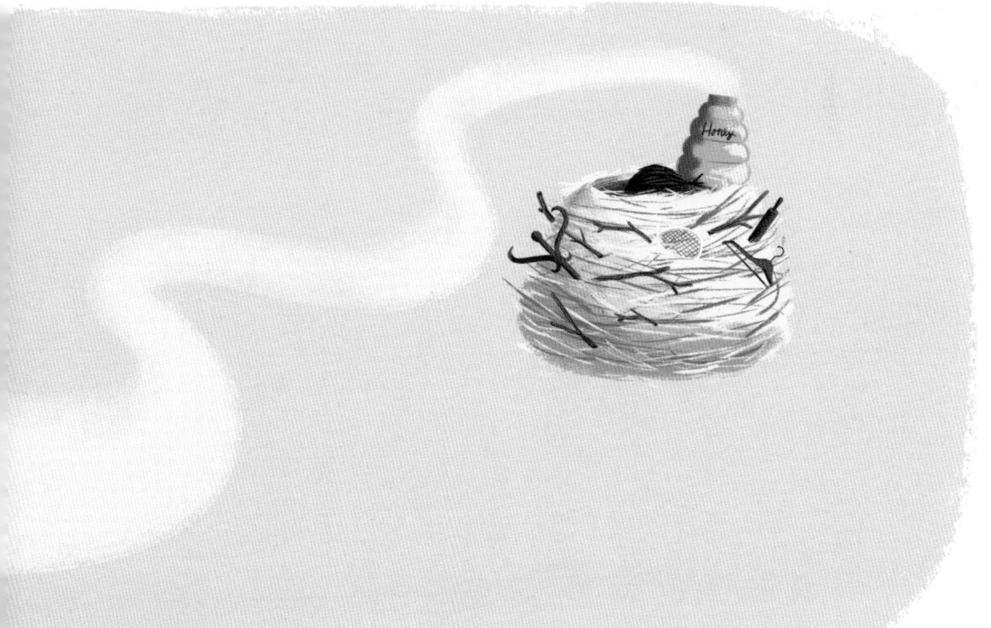
Honey

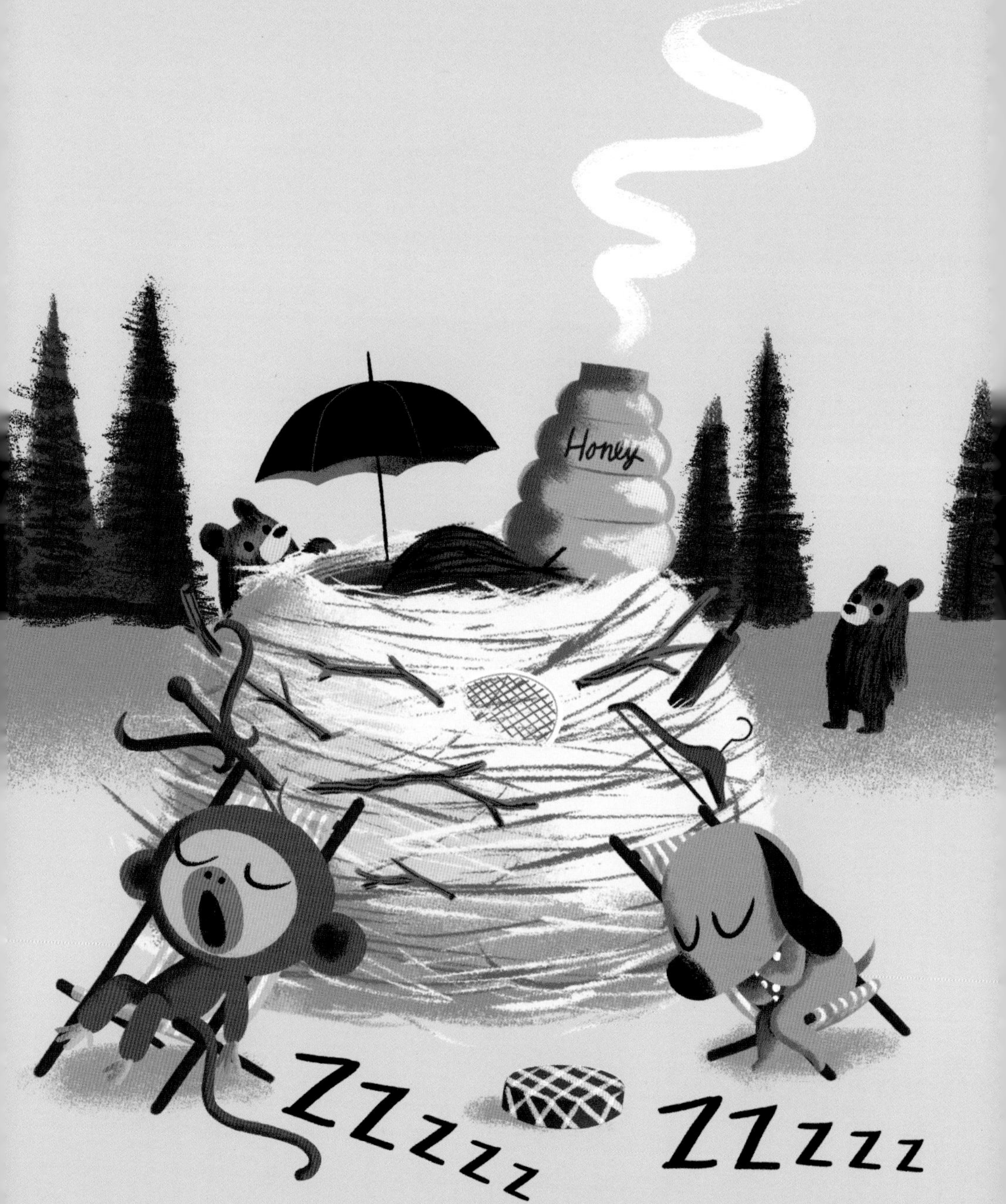
Honey
ZZzzzz
ZZzzzz

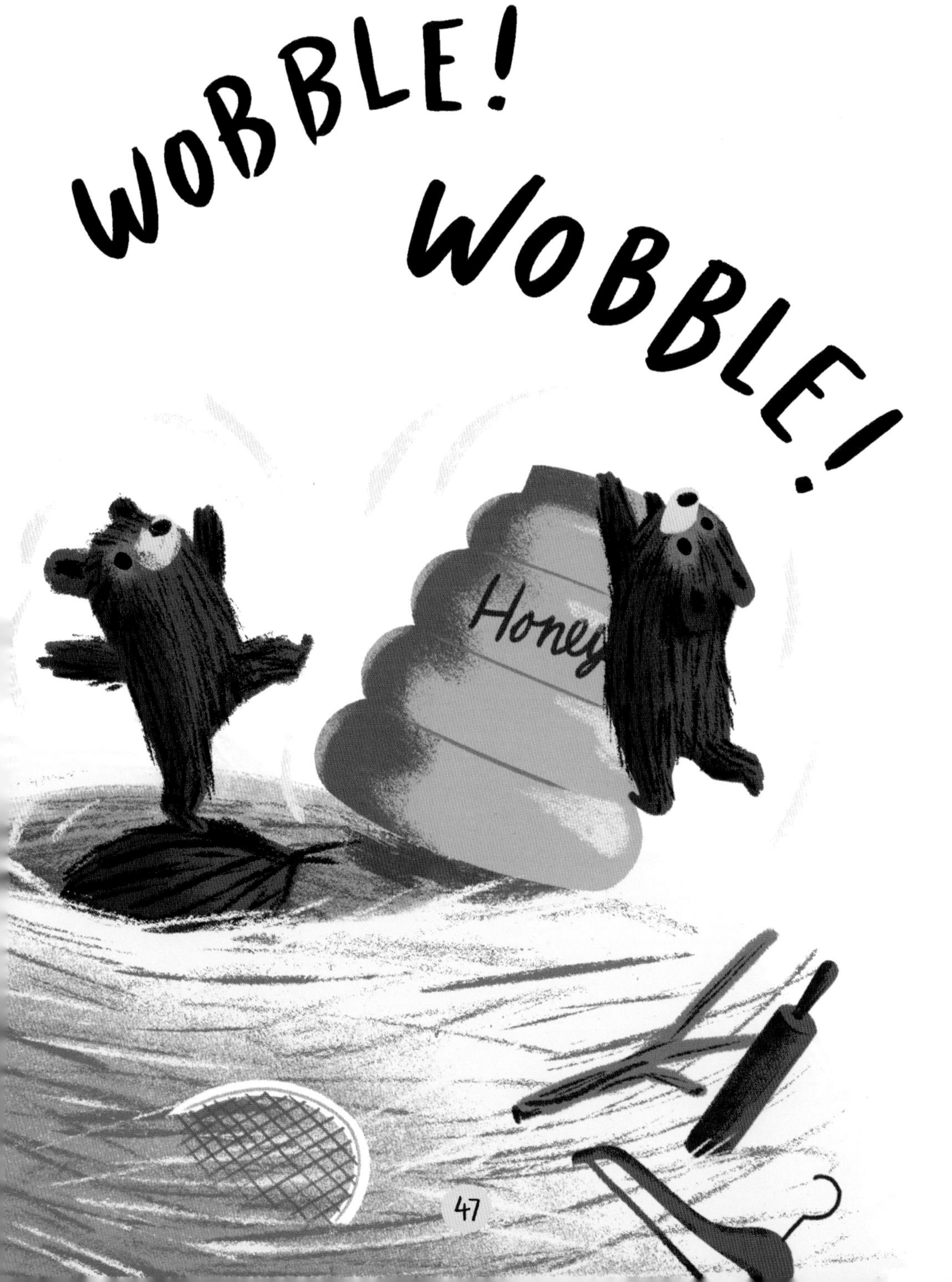
WOBBLE!
WOBBLE!
Honey

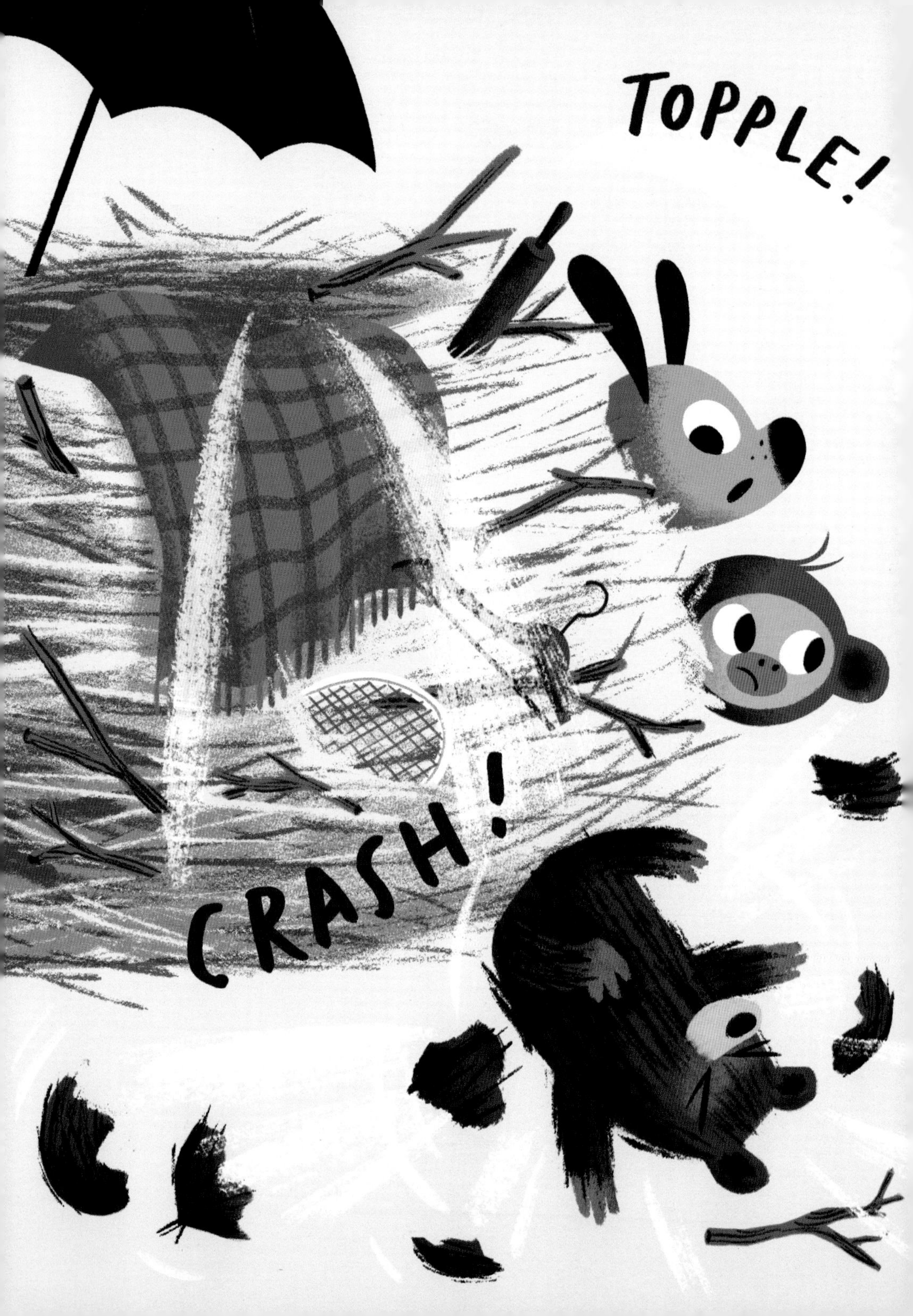
TOPPLE!
CRASH!

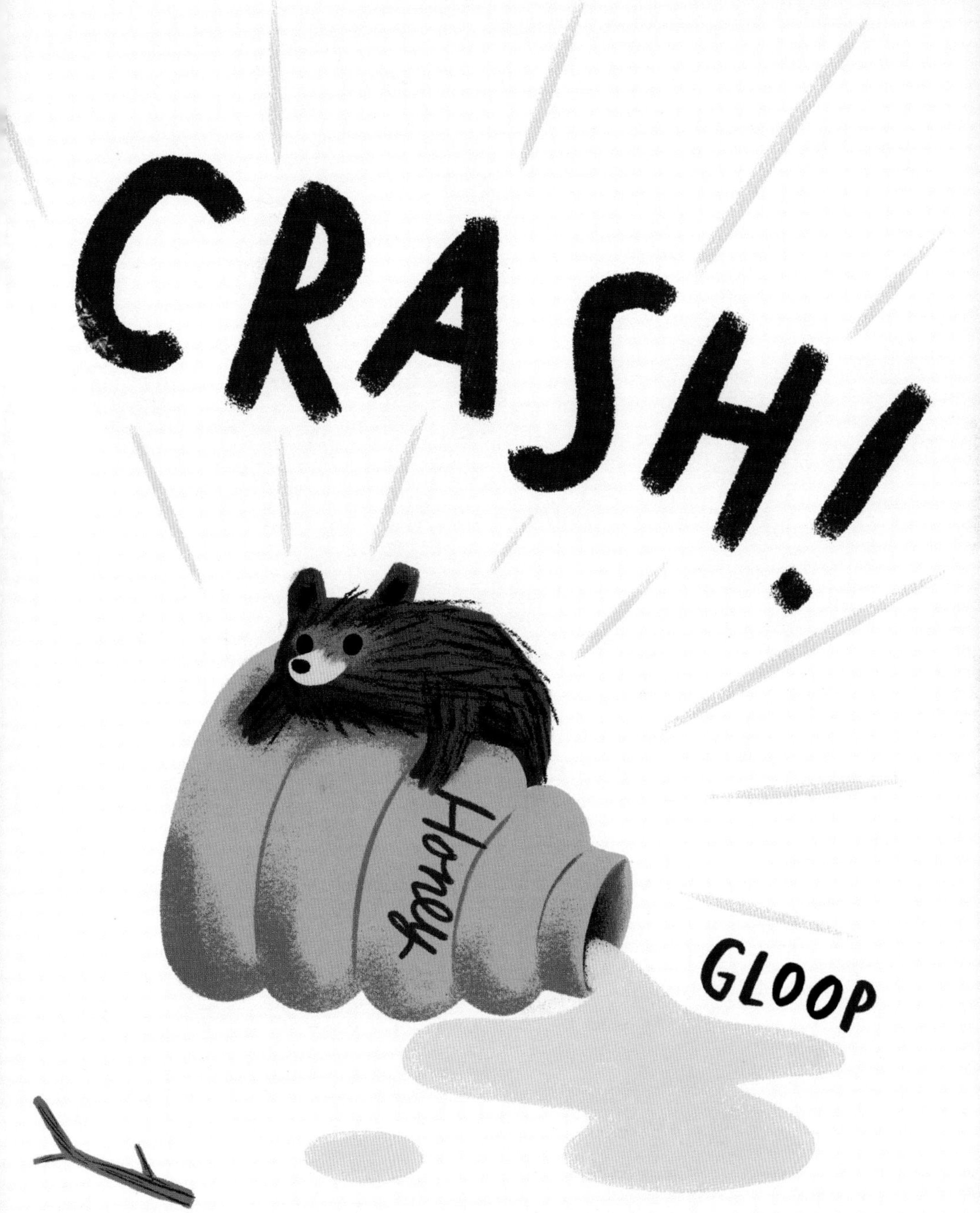
CRASH!
Honey
GLOOP

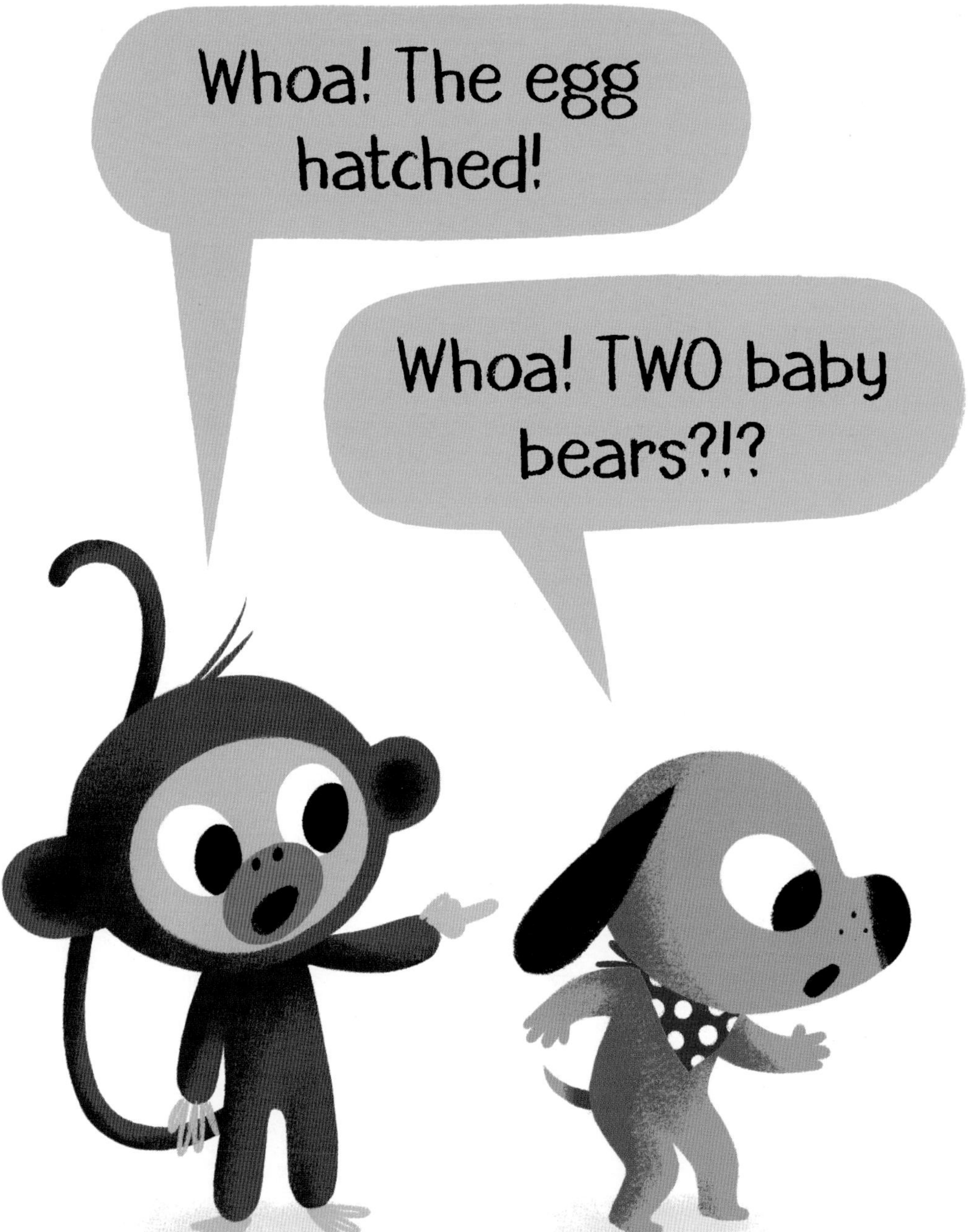
Whoa! The egg hatched!
Whoa! TWO baby bears?!?

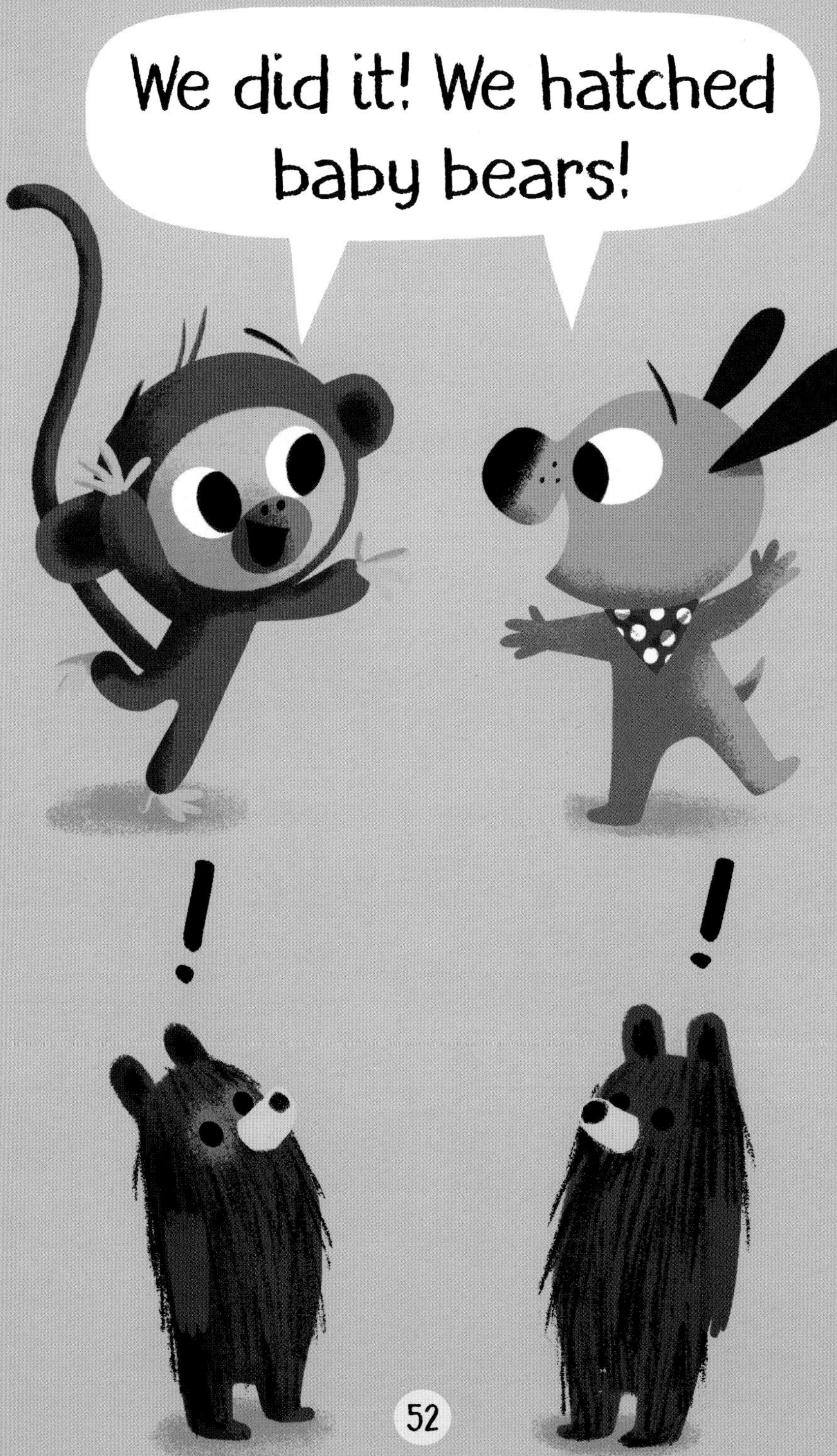
We did it! We hatched baby bears!
!
!

We love you,
baby bears!

Bye-bye,
baby
bears!

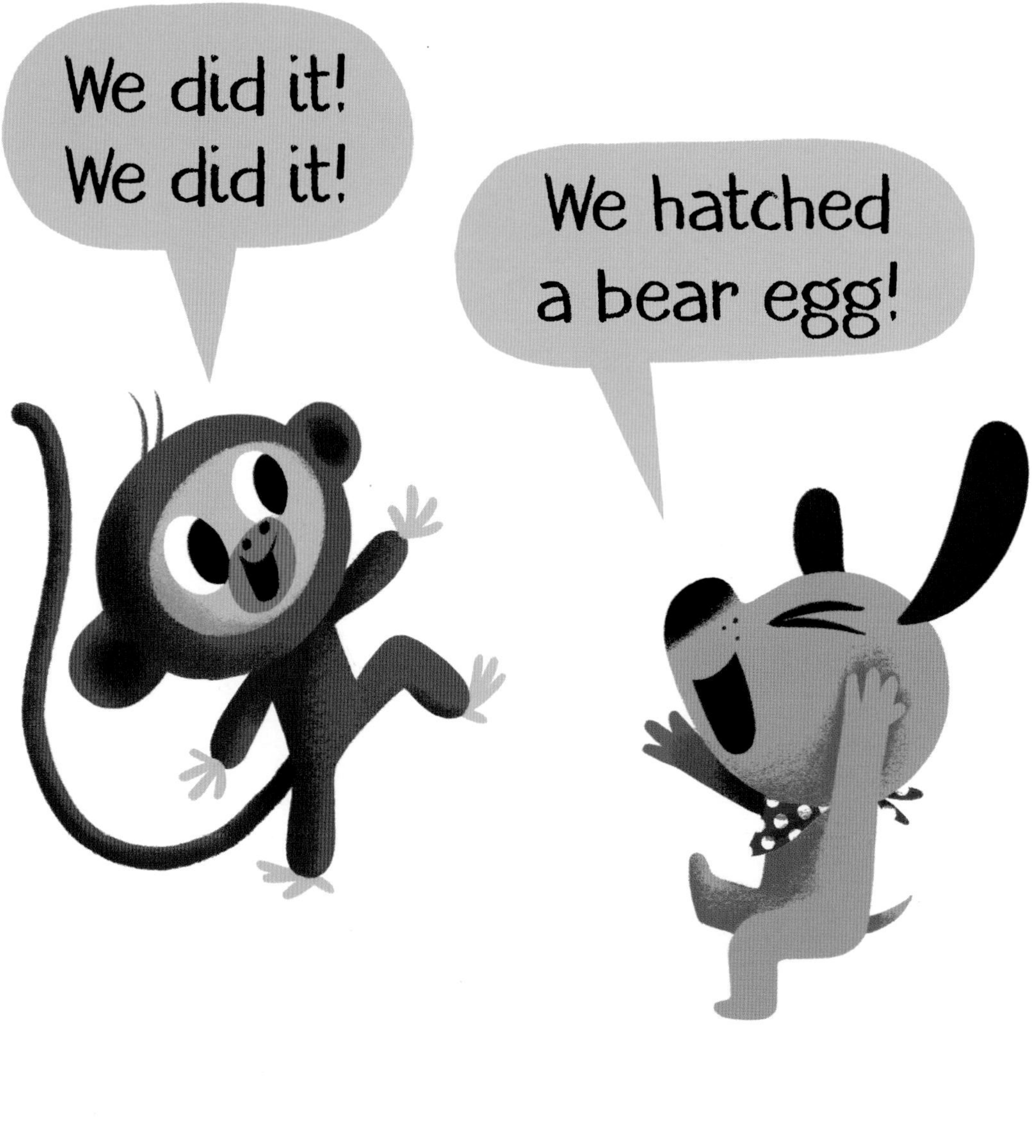
We did it!
We did it!
We hatched
a bear egg!

That was so much
fun! What should
we do next?

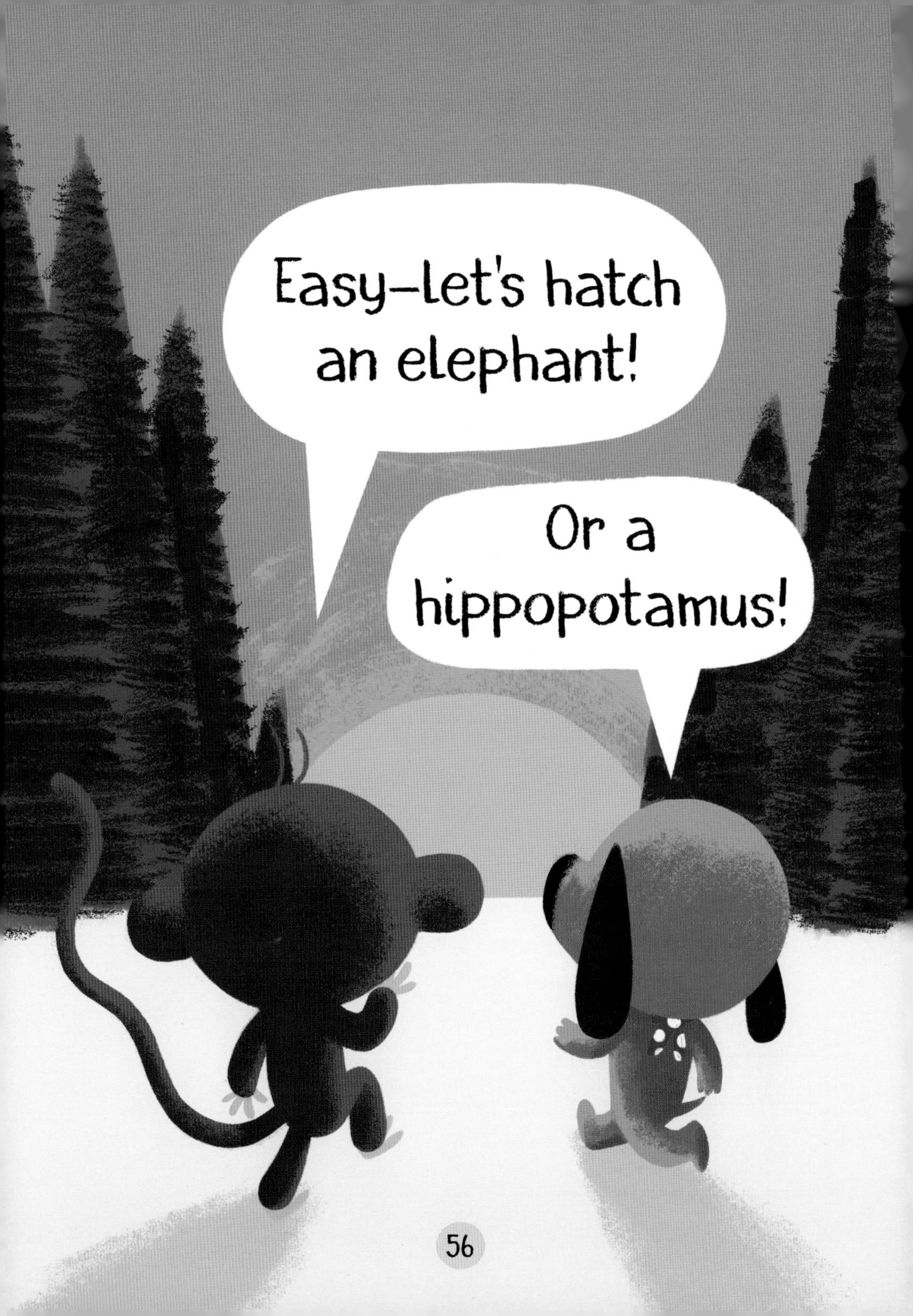
Easy—let's hatch an elephant!
Or a hippopotamus!

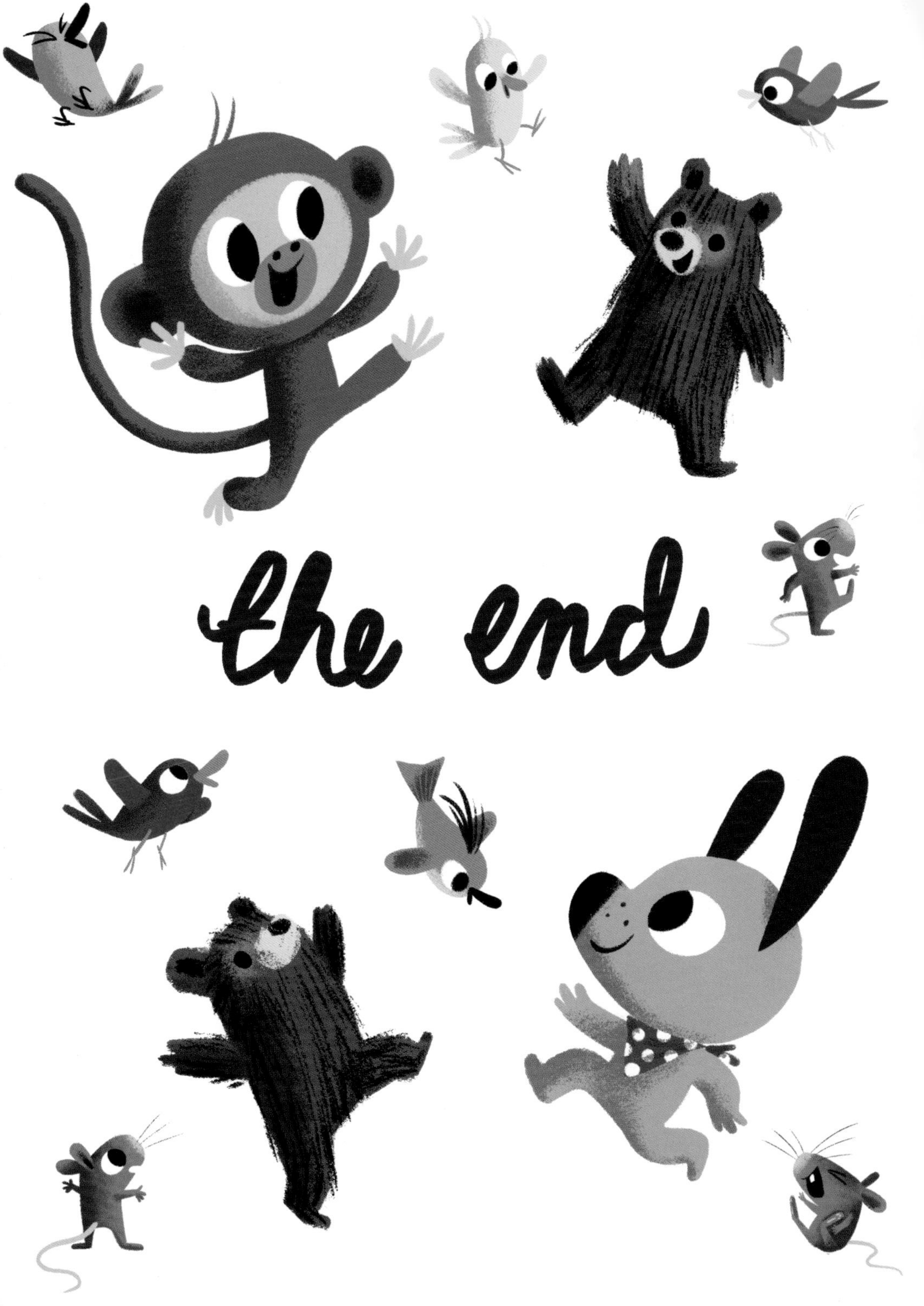
the end

If you think THIS book was funny, you'll love these!

Don't miss a single adventure starring Bobo and Pup-Pup!

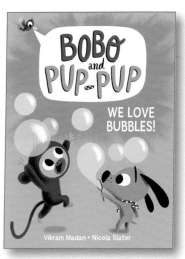

BOBO and PUP-PUP
WE LOVE BUBBLES!
Vikram Madan • Nicola Slater

BOBO and PUP-PUP
LET'S MAKE CAKE!
Vikram Madan • Nicola Slater

BOBO and PUP-PUP
THE FUNNY BOOK
HEE! HEE!
Vikram Madan • Nicola Slater

BOBO and PUP-PUP
HATCH AN EGG
Vikram Madan • Nicola Slater

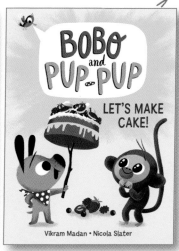

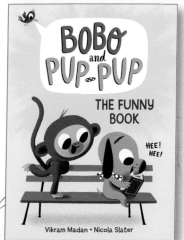

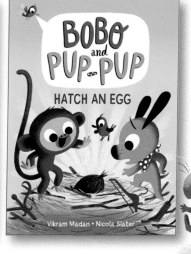

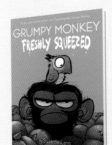

Vikram Madan grew up in India, where he really wanted to be a cartoonist but ended up an engineer. After a long time, he realized that what he really wants to do is hatch ideas for funny books. His self-illustrated book *A Hatful of Dragons: And More Than 13.8 Billion Other Funny Poems* was selected as a Best Book by *Kirkus Reviews*, the New York Public Library, and Bank Street College of Education, among other honors. He is also the author-illustrator of the graphic reader *Owl and Penguin*. He lives in Seattle with his family. Visit him at VikramMadan.com.

Nicola Slater lives with her family in the wild and windy north of England. She has illustrated many middle-grade novels and picture books, including *Where Is My Pink Sweater?* (which she also wrote), *Leaping Lemmings!, A Skunk in My Bunk!,* and Margaret Wise Brown's *Manners,* a Little Golden Book. In her spare time she likes looking at animals, camping in the rain, and tickling her children. You can follow her on Twitter at @nicolaslater.